*Europe*

# *Europe after the Rain*

## Alan Burns

CALDER

CALDER PUBLICATIONS
an imprint of

ALMA BOOKS LTD
3 Castle Yard
Richmond
Surrey TW10 6TF
United Kingdom
www.calderpublications.com

*Europe after the Rain* first published by John Calder (Publishers) Ltd
in 1965
This edition first published by Calder Publications in 2019

Cover design by Will Dady

Printed and bound by CPI Group (UK) Ltd, Croydon, CR0 4YY

ISBN: 978-0-7145-4916-3

# Contents

Europe after the Rain                                    1
*Chapter 1*                                              3
*Chapter 2*                                             13
*Chapter 3*                                             23
*Chapter 4*                                             31
*Chapter 5*                                             41
*Chapter 6*                                             49
*Chapter 7*                                             55
*Chapter 8*                                             59
*Chapter 9*                                             63
*Chapter 10*                                            73
*Chapter 11*                                            81
*Chapter 12*                                            89
*Chapter 13*                                            95
*Chapter 14*                                           103
*Chapter 15*                                           111

*Note on the Text*                                     115

TO CAROL

*Europe after*
*the Rain*

# Chapter 1

WE WERE APPROACHING the river. The modern bridge had been demolished, a wooden one constructed. Passengers were ordered to get out and walk across. The way led from the metalled surface of the road over deeply frayed planks. Seventy yards away the permanent bridge, massive steel and concrete, was still half completed. Danger threatened the wooden bridge – ice pressed against the log piles supporting it. Explosions broke the silence as a soldier with a pole placed packages on the ice. "It's moving," she said. Slowly the ice pack oscillated and a large piece broke away to be carried by the current fast beneath the bridge.

In the bus, all the seats were occupied. "Don't worry," she said. "When the control comes, the people will have to get out." Two passengers could not find their tickets. They were taken off to some sort of centre, or so I was told. Genuine passengers were driven to the outskirts of the frontier town. The driver was pleasant enough: "Of course it is bad here, but not so bad as you might think."

At the first building, I asked her: "Won't it be closed? It's already well after seven." "Someone is bound to be on duty." A light shone. "You were right, someone is here." In a room lit by a bulb, a middle-aged woman sat knitting. She did not glance at us. I was left alone with her; a man came in; the three sat in silence; I wrapped in my coat.

The girl returned. "Drink?" "I don't drink," she replied. "Never?" "I don't like alcohol." The man asked her to dance; she glanced down at his boots, and danced with him. "You'll have to dance with all of them. Let's leave – it's no use waiting. I'll pay the bill." The man made a movement with his hand. "We must pay the bill." He did not reply.

We were separated. I objected: "She is in my care until she has contacted her family." We had to stand in front of a desk. She understood that the words used were a message of welcome. They appeared to have a most enjoyable conversation. He walked backwards and forwards; I waited – I knew I would have to wait.

The rooms were littered with paper and rubbish. Room after room showed the same sight. A photograph lay in the dust on the floor of one room – she picked it up, glanced at it, then flicked it back to its former place. "Upstairs it's a bit risky," she warned. "Have you got a torch?" Everything had gone, even the floorboards. The staircase to the top floor was planks battened together. "That's the door," she said. "I shall wait for you here." The door opened slightly; the eye of a girl. "Do you mind waiting a little? Someone isn't really dressed yet." She showed no marked sign of being other than healthy. "We were two patients to a bed. My fellow patient was a man who died. They left him with me for two days before taking him away." There was no trace of hysteria. "It was nice of you to come."

We walked fast in a strong cold wind, among loose stuff lying about. A viaduct led to the destroyed bridge; we ran down stone steps to reach the street – whole steps were missing, the gaps protected by wire. Single walls crashed. Music sounded from a church – people with dogs waited at the entrance; the stairway was packed with a stationary crowd of listeners. Two new trolleybuses were being tested. I counted thirty wooden huts. Girls stood in a circle singing a patriotic song. She would not join them.

We knocked. We said we could not stay.

We went to two cinemas.

Someone called for her. She discussed her plans. "As a matter of fact, I have not got any plan." "You have names and addresses." "I am probably standing on a dead body." She bought two and a half pounds of sweets. Anyone could buy sweets. Everyone did a little buying and selling. Loot. Though there was little left. There were other ways. Casual labour received high wages. She did private work in the evenings. Quality work. One house was famous. The owner sang those songs. She sang the one we had heard in the street.

At the orphanage we were told that orphans arrived in a number of ways. "The police find them. Or neighbours bring them. Some arrive on their own." A boy of twelve had just arrived. He presented himself. A woman came with two children – she was their neighbour; their father had had an accident. They were disinfected and medically examined. They went through the hands of an examiner – a heavy woman with a strong face, cold, distrustful; a woman on the other side of the writing desk. She tested the children. She showed us her equipment. "I have to carry out my tests. Most of the children are of normal intelligence. The history of each is written down. When it is a case of a brother and sister, this is marked on both cards. The building has three floors. Each floor is isolated to prevent the spread of infection. Children from three to eight are encouraged to play with toys." "Who sends them toys?" "And there are kitchens, and there are laundries." The interview, though it produced no useful information, was most pleasant. There were no armed guards or admittance permits. She was a member of the aristocracy. We could speak direct. "What do you want? Where would you like to go? No, it is too dangerous." "Someone must make a start." "I shall see what I can do." We saw the kitchens. We tasted the food. It was the same. The food was available. They achieved the maximum flavour by careful cooking. "A soup well made is the best means of deriving the most benefit." The shops were filled with food. The children got milk for breakfast twice a week. A fine piece of work.

A boy. The sun. The windows. The rays of the sun streamed direct from the heavens. The boy talked to her: "We got on a boat, a train, they caught us, back you go, they bought us tickets, we hid till the train went, we came out, why are you not on that train? It's gone, it's your fault, you told us the wrong time. Wait here for the next train. Before we started out we collected anything we could find, and our friends gave us things. When we got hungry we sold everything." They asked his name. No one knew his parents – they had disappeared, absolutely; he wasn't sure of his name – it had been signed away to someone else. They took his clothes, bathed him, turned him over, gave him other clothes. He asked for his own. She said: "With very little you do a great deal, and do it well." On our way to the dining room the boy stopped us: "I'm glad you've come. I thought I had been forgotten."

Up two flights of steps, a room: forty feet by forty feet, thirteen feet high. The walls and ceiling were painted white. On each wall, a fresco: undamaged cities, a dancer, an eagle five feet square, done in black on scarlet, no intention of flight, massive legs – it was not an eagle. A continuous table, along three sides of the room, had been laid for supper: plates of excellent ham, thin slices of sausage made from meat, fish in oil, boiled eggs, salted and spiced, various salads and cheese. But eating would not take place for some time. Sweet biscuits of several kinds were placed on the table. Conversation started. They recalled the tortures in the building. An undercurrent of recklessness. "We can stand anything, if you know what that means." We had to ask questions. It had been agreed that I was to remain. I asked about the boy. "I don't know whether I should tell you. It was done without my knowledge. These young people. If I had known I should not have allowed it." I noticed her eating the biscuits. "Look at the roof – just above the room with the high windows. You see? The yellow tiles are new. Crawling and working on a steep roof. A drop of forty feet from the gutter." A hasty whispering took place. It was time for us to go. "Do you mind waiting? We shall have to give you an escort – that is, if you wish to return."

We drove back across the bridge. The river ran past the town from south-east to north-west. We went round two sides of an open square. The doors of the car would not close properly. The driver demanded to be paid. I refused.

I bought her a belt for her birthday – a broad band of lemon yellow. She said: "Today is a day. I don't notice any difference from other days. We visited the blind. Nurses gave their lives. I have no time. I have work to do. But now I must go to sleep."

We had identical conversations with high-placed officials. I asked if we had a chance of finding the right direction. They laughed. She said afterwards: "If you overwork them, they collapse. Something happens. They break down."

They worked by candlelight. The electric cable had not been relaid. Hesitation was not tolerated. Each was required to correct mistakes. The standard of attention demanded was high. Questions were snapped at them, incorrect attitudes eliminated.

Police headquarters had been repaired. Electric lights functioned. I was standing at the back of the office when she entered. She explained the reason for her visit. It was not always easy to understand what she was trying to say. She would have to have lessons. She had no map. She tried to draw a map.

For years she had lived an abnormal life. She had been intensively trained. This had lowered her capacity to concentrate. She had formed habits of thought. Here was a powerful and unknown force. Her structure had been completely destroyed, in blood and burning. The structure of this girl was a new and unknown factor in history. It would be known only in the future. It would be something quite different from what her teachers had intended.

I had a haircut, a shave; my suit pressed, I collected clean clothes from the laundry. At my door a shoe-cleaner waited; he cleaned my shoes, and with his assistance I bought some books, locks and bolts, a basket of bread, a pail of eggs, cakes and flowers. I put the cakes and flowers in her room. The flower shops were filled with flowers. No one was allowed to have more than one room – few had more than the corner of a room. They needed a few flowers, and rich cakes with layers of thick cream; twenty shops sold such cakes – cakes had never been so rich or so plentiful – every woman who could made them at home and sold them to the shops.

Carrying my case, I walked back to the hotel. I had a pleasant surprise. I had not expected to be allowed into my room, but the hall porter handed me the key. On entering,

I found her things lying about. There was no handle to the door of the room, so that, should I have closed it, I could not have opened it again. Someone knocked on the door and pushed it open: "Remember me?" I saw a young girl – I knew that I knew her well, and that she was someone I really liked, but I could not place her. Asking her to be seated, I went to my suitcase to fiddle about with its contents while I was trying to remember who she was. "How did you know I was here?" I asked. I remembered buying her flowers a few days before. "There are lots of things I should like you to explain – for example, the flower shops." She replied: "Flowers are good. Every office has a canteen. The hundredth trolleybus has been repaired. Thank you for the flowers. They are a great help." "And the man who cleans my shoes?" "Offices have canteens." She showed me hundreds of duplicated typewritten sheets. She handed me one. Her views were sane, but they were not her own.

I asked her questions. We had continually to change the place to avoid attracting attention. Carts hauled away rubble; these vehicles were long and narrow – wedge-shaped troughs – the sides were loose planks; the wheels had been taken from army lorries, as had the tyres, balloon tyres, and the ball-bearing axles. The standing figures, in groups of twos and threes, watched. She made some futile remarks about them. She was reading as she walked along, licking a finger tip, turning over a clinging page. It was late. The building was being cleaned and repainted – they were cleaning the high crystal windows. We discussed *Gone With the Wind*. I tried to attend. The crowd was too dense. I studied the outside of the buildings: house joined to house in a continuous row. The height of the rooms was eleven feet, and the floors were one foot thick – the houses were dead and derelict fortresses; vitality in one or two rooms, warm and lit. This was the heat of the life of the town.

We sat on benches along the walls – the centre of the room had been cleared for dancing. We played draughts with the board between us on the bench. The dancing was due to start. I mentioned the songs. She said something to one of the others, who, immediately, but without interrupting his game, started a song. The girls sang as a choir, the boys played instruments. They broke off to gaze at me. A hurried talk, then three of them formed themselves into a row, and three stood behind them. By keeping close they made a compact group, their bodies rigid; they kept time with sharp marionette movements of hand and head. It was effective, even menacing, but I could not interpret it. I knew it portrayed something powerful, and perhaps reckless. She said that the choir prepared concerts for its own pleasure – it had never performed outside the building. While they were singing, she cut strips of coloured paper and stuck them onto a piece of white card. She made an intricate paper box: a square building freshly painted white. She talked to me. She had found some books belonging to her father – her trouble was where to hide them. It was not easily done. They had strict control over the bridge. She had taken the youngest and prettiest girl, and they had pretended. The books were stored and completely lost; she could not find where she had hidden them. She became hysterical. We moved to another room. The windows were holes in the walls; the plaster had fallen away; there were gaps in the floors. Her two brothers had been killed, her father had disappeared – she wanted to get back to a normal life. "I was mad with joy. I could not understand it. I thought they wanted to kill just as I wanted to kill. After this I do not believe anything. My brothers were sent to work in the forests. I don't know where. I have not heard of them since." Forty people were jammed in the room – everyone was compelled to stand upright. They formed against the walls, leaving a small square free. Her group was to sing as a choir. There were nine of them. I had a special interest in them. There was some bustling in the next room, and from time to time the connecting door opened. Then it was flung open and she ran in, dressed in odd bits of coloured material and a few ribbons, in an effort to resemble a gay costume. She sang the same song and finished with an attempt to dance. She had shown great ingenuity in using coloured paper for her costume. She wore a coloured paper cap, and concealed her hands from everyone.

In the morning I found her with the children, carrying steaming pails of soup across the courtyard. I watched her cross the cobbled stone yard. The steam was dense. She was in charge of ladling out the soup, and could not be disturbed. The old woman told me that she could not be interrupted. Through a glass door on one side: the old woman in a black jacket, in the dim light of a box-like room, on and on – motionless body. She got up from her chair, opened the glass door and invited me to enter: "It is warmer here." I said I wished to speak to the girl. She needed help. "We give help," the woman replied. "We have a list. We make enquiries. We have had contests in swimming with eight hundred spectators." I said I had to see the girl on official business. I was informed that she was engaged: I would have to wait. There were several men there – they seemed worried, and whispered together. A man walked from the room. The woman spoke to me:

"What shall I tell her?" "Tell her I want to see her." I heard a voice behind a closed door: "Who is there?" I went in. "This is no place." The room was half a room, screened – two beds, a small table, a coke stove with a pan on top. "It's too dark to read here. We have a window, but it is boarded up – the boards are warmer in winter." I replied: "So far the winter has been mild." "Twice I have lost everything. This time I hope I shall be able to keep what I have got. Nothing is going to be stolen from here." She showed me the bread she had made. The walls were decorated with paper figures from fairy tales; the home seemed so rich with things of wood made by hand. "I am sorry I came so late," I said, "and now I have come at an awkward time." "I'm afraid I must break off this conversation." "I hope I am not making things difficult for you. I know where you intend to go. It is a prohibited area. No foreigners allowed." "I don't need you. I can travel alone." "They are at war. You have heard of their attempts to pacify." "There are all sorts of rumours." "How do you manage alone?" "It is difficult. I have to fight. I have to say to myself loudly and continuously that I can fight and win – I can save myself. When you failed to come, I sent a message that you were not to come back." "What happened then?" "You came." There was a bed with one thin blanket. We lay on the bed. "Show me your hands." She held out her hands. I wore my coat. We discussed my proposal to visit the town where her father had last been seen. It was a question of transport, the state of the road, the actual condition of the surface of the road, the presence of bandits. Buses had been stopped and the passengers robbed.

# Chapter 2

THE TRANSPORT ARRIVED. The driver was ready to take the risk. The car had a hood, and planks on each side; we were wrapped in blankets. The hooded interior was a small room. We faced each other and carried on a conversation. We were going to the town where her father – so she had been told – had been recently buried.

All bridges were broken. The front wheels were over a trench in the road. We got help; with concrete blocks we built a way across the trench. It was dark. We clambered out of the hooded wagon. We quarrelled. I was not clear what it was all about. We fought. She did not want to be forced. There was silence. I needed help. "We are lucky to be in a town. I shall get help from somewhere." A clock struck nine; the street was empty – no light shone from the houses. "I shall find a place." She remained in the wagon. She called out: "I want some hot tea. Can I have some tea?" "No." "Please speak. I like to hear it." "Tea?" "Do you understand?" "I'll get you some tea." "Don't leave me." "I must look for a place: we must get somewhere to sleep – otherwise we will have to answer more questions."

The streets were quiet. I found a man, I argued with him, he directed me. The place was closed. I smashed down a door. A man with a gun waited. I told him what we wanted. He did nothing. The wind was blowing sleet. I passed a church tower. Cavalry clattered by, followed by men on foot carrying long, straight scythes; the wind bent the peacock feathers in their caps and the sleet beat on our faces as we tramped through the slush.

We stayed in her father's house. In the living room were two beds, a round table with a lace centrepiece, a carpet on a polished floor. We were welcomed as guests. The caretaker heated the stove; his wife prepared some tea, eggs and bread and butter. The room was not warm enough. The old man took the best bed out of the living room and carried it into the next room. It was two o'clock in the morning. On the wall was a large oil painting. Whether it was an original or a copy was open to doubt. The point interested me. I had noticed two indifferent paintings hung in the living room: old portraits of generals, or priests – leaders of some kind.

She asked about the doctor who had attended her father. "That fellow is not – the doctor is no good. He ought to be kept in prison, but, like the last time, he will be let out after a few months."

The doctor was dead. She called on his deputy. It was a huge organization. The deputy's assistant saw her; she learnt that her father had suffered from tuberculosis in an acute form and from a condition of the heart. There had been one curious feature – deep-rooted, fascinating.

We had coffee. A baker's assistant carried on his head two large wooden trays loaded with cakes, pastries, loaves. Hot milk poured steaming into glasses. She ate four excellent cakes; reaching for another cake, she almost upset her coffee over me. She was under twenty, illiterate, completely untrained. She had been taught a certain occupation. "When did you learn," I asked her, "that you were going to be sent here?" "Last November. I was told that it had been agreed that you were to take me." "How long will you stay?" "I am supposed to stay for ten days, and in that time find the grave. But I'm ill, not fit for work, so I must look after myself. I know there is no grave. I should like to see him back, but it is not safe for him. People disappear – no one knows where they go. Probably it will change; I don't know what to do. I should like to stay here, but I don't know how long they will allow me to. Certain people are not seen in the streets any more, and so it is forgotten that they are in control." "If it is a question of your father—" "I am not interested. I must get a good job. I have found jobs in flower shops; many times it has happened, but the work… I cannot get used to it. The reason is clear: poverty is a sin; the good man is rewarded – he is successful. I shall found a new kind of institution for orphans. It will be a garden. Any country would be proud to possess such an orphanage. The building will be designed to give the children the maximum sunlight when indoors. The children will be poorly clad and ill-shod, they will be kept in a massive building with automatically regulated furnaces; the ovens will be on the same high level of modern design." I preferred not to ask where she had learnt all this.

I took her back to her wooden room. She lifted her coat; she had no clothing underneath. "I have access to stocks of clothing. Would you like me to treat you differently?" She said she had no need of money. I asked her if the others had money. She said yes. "If you worked hard, would you get the chance to earn more?" She was not sure about this – first she said yes, then no. I asked her how many there were in her family. "One." "I did not ask you how many now – I know that; I wish to know how many you were." "Five." "And how many are left?" Silence. "How many?" "One." "And the others?" "Gone." "Children?" "Yes." "Did the others die?" This produced some confusion. Experience had taught me to be cautious about accepting statements at their face value. Information had to be extracted. She sat there thinking, preoccupied with survival. She divided her attention between watching me and having some game with crumbs of cake. She was indifferent – no emotion – yet I was asking questions often of the most intimate nature. It had a sinister meaning. "I gave you a fresh set of clothing, but you will not help me – you sit and do nothing." "Give me better clothes and I will help – don't give me these rags, don't lock the door." I made sure the door was locked behind me. Everything had turned to iron – six million pieces of iron, with appendages.

I woke her up; I stood by the door. "My friend," I spoke quietly. "Who are you?" She got out of bed. "Why are you here?" "You said you were too ill to work; you must be looked after – you are going on a holiday – now behave yourself." "What can I take with me?" "Personal belongings; no furniture." "I have no furniture." "It is not important." Her fingers were clumsy; she fumbled with the buttons. I noticed her long and curved lashes. I kicked her clothes into the corner of the room. A steel comb dragged through her hair. "My eyes hurt." "You are ill," I said. "You need hospital treatment." "I must get a new coat – I'll sell my coat and buy a new one; there are new long coats on the market." I was wearing my overcoat, as the place was unheated. "Get in." She climbed into the bath – the level of the water was below the knee – she splashed the water over herself, trying to cover her body. "Could I have some more water?" "Not allowed; scrub yourself clean." She stepped out of the bath: she looked cold. I gave her back her clothes and she put them on. I felt the twitch of my lips as I turned away and started to lock the shutters. "Why do you block out the air?" The windows were barred; a metal shade protected the light. I handed her a slice of buttered bread. She put the bread on the floor. I stood over her, my face irritable with impatience. "Take it. Quick." She couldn't hold it properly – she was cold. I watched in silence. "Get back to bed." The room contained nothing but a bed, a chair, a tin bath. No pictures, no book, no jug of water, no calendar, no mirror. Her lips were counting numbers. I heard someone pass in the corridor outside. I asked her how old she was and whether she liked the food. She picked up the chair and came towards me; I twisted it out of her hands – it was too heavy for her.

She lay back, face upwards, looking at the ceiling, her face a piece of paper. She could not make the effort to stand up. She tried to avoid contact with me by turning towards the wall. "Do what you're told – go and get ready." "No." "It's for your own good." "I don't want to – you can't make me." But she began to pick up her few clothes from the floor. "I can't go; I have a horror of hospitals: I once went to the doctor – he wouldn't examine me; I had no friends – no one – I had had my teeth out, all my teeth drawn. My father paid the bill – it had to be paid; the doctor came to see me: he asked how I was; I said I was well, and he went away." She was waiting to see what I would do – for something to happen which would prevent her having to go. "I worked in the kitchens; I had swollen legs – you can see they are still bad. My father said I grew too quickly; I should not have done so. While I was working. I drank a lot of water, and I ate boiled fish, but the kitchens – all the steam and heat – it put you off your food, and my nerves were bad; I tried ointments, I put black paste on the painful parts, I had advice from everyone, I was told to eat stews and soup, to avoid the terrible heat and the dampness. I still use drops twice a day." She stooped close to the floor, unable to go on, waiting for me to move. When I left her, she lay on the low table, her head pointing towards the door.

Hurrying downstairs, I was delayed by men carrying out bodies: they forced past me; one shoved a fist into my face. They grinned as the bodies came out. I looked straight ahead. They did not appear to know that I had been living in the house. Crowds on the stairs filled every foot of room; trunks had been left in the hall half-packed. Fugitives who faced exposure filled the hall with shouting to be allowed out, but the uniformed traitors dragged them from the door. At the door stood the caretaker of the building – the man who had welcomed us and made us tea. "Without exception all are to be turned back." I tried to touch his hand, to get closer to him and explain. "All persons are to remain here. No exceptions whatsoever." No one could deprive them of their sport: the scenes of fear. They forced the girl down on her hands and knees and made her scrub the stairs with acid preparations which bit into the skin; she was surrounded by jostling men – they put a scrubbing brush into her hand, splashed it well with acid. "Now you need more water." They slung a bucket of filthy water over her, then jerked her up by the wrists and made her show her hands.

They were intent on their enjoyment. The stairs were black with happy onlookers. I did not know one of them. She stared up at them; her mouth could not keep still. I got to the door and spoke to the man guarding it. "I must speak to you at once." "Who are you? I don't know you." I told him what I knew about the girl and her father. "If they discover who she is, it means her life. Certain information may help; so may money. I told her to ask me for money. I don't know her real name – I have no idea what will happen to her." "She is one of many. Things will get worse. She won't be heard of again." He gave me a paper with instructions. "Someone will come within a week. If no one comes, destroy it – it is all over."

The doors were kept locked; we were shut in for twelve hours; we were examined – those who were ill were dragged into one room. They had lists. She was one of those taken away by lorry. I should have stayed and searched for her, but I was not sure how long they would allow me to remain. The main thing was that I should not lose contact with her. Everything was stolen, mirrors shot to pieces, the paintings ripped with knives, plates and glasses smashed – all with the utmost indifference. They telephoned for more lorries.

Food. The movements of waiters. I learnt. Those mysterious persons. While at lunch one came to see me. "Is there anything I can do for you?" Certainly, though his face… He conferred. It was a question of transport. "Is there a lorry?" "Yes. One of my men will go with you."

An empty lorry. My luggage was placed on the seat beside the driver; I chose the most comfortable place in the back. Soon the back of the lorry was crammed – every space was filled with bodies and cases. The luggage remained on the seat. It was an order.

Later, when I had made it clear that I was going to cooperate, they placed a car at my disposal. It was built for military purposes, but I was not going to miss the opportunity of having a car. The seats were cut and torn. A person lay across the seats, and had to be thrown out.

The armoured cars I was compelled to follow were scarred by war; each carried a pennant – three different pennants – three divisions. Their commander greeted me in the friendliest way, so that I felt I need not worry too much over whether or not I was travelling in the right direction.

The road was a straight strip between high hedges; the rays of the winter sun were unexpectedly warm. When we stopped at an empty house, people came to look at us – old people arrived in procession, women whose houses had been burnt down, who had gone for months without food, saving so that they could rebuild, faces dull purple, women blood-red tipped, men faded. They brought us tea, which was excellent. They talked about their houses, but these people could not be reached; until they had their own homes, they could not hope. The range of food carried by the convoy, and which they allowed me to share, was limited, though it included some remarkable delicacies.

The missing-persons office had a new wooden roof – light yellow – the only roof that had been repaired. The office was closed. I was not concerned. I had a good road, a fast car, a reckless driver. The troops carried in the armoured cars went round systematically burning and blowing up buildings. They had sixty-four houses, then they had three. The troops repaired two. They helped them get going again. I asked the commander: "What about the people who used to live in these houses – are they still here?" "No. Deported to work in factories. Others drift back, others have been murdered, burnt." "I don't understand why." "You don't know them." His face showed signs of strain. "We brought them thirty tons of DDT. We organized squads. We broke the back of epidemics. Without DDT, typhus would spread without any hope of stopping it. That powder is one of the best things we have done. The girl? It is one case only. With migrations, changing populations and fresh troops in the district, new batches of cases are continually being notified, and we have no idea of the number of unreported cases. We need help badly. We are cut off here. Can't you do something? Are you content to sit and take notes?" "Today I am going to visit a person who, I believe, is living in the district, and who may be able to help in tracing her." "Perhaps you can get us some medicine." I heard him say that, and I decided to do what I could to help him.

The troops had gone. The house was in darkness. A woman with brown hair welcomed me; she couldn't sit still – leaning her face against mine, she continued to tremble. She started to tell about the hanging – she tried to explain why she got the words twisted, but she could not. She held the light; the words got lost. I waited. Her thin face... she lived in the dark. She sat beside the light and started to talk. Soldiers had been in her home. She had tried to take care. There had been men outside the house – she had seen them in the street. A knock on the door: we have four prisoners... could you go to another house – of course not. The prisoners came – the most terrible people; it was painful to hear their treatment; when she complained she was told that soon they would be going home – with a rope. Through the window she saw them, their hands tied: four men; they were led aside. It was not that I was indifferent – I was not – but I was calm; I had no part of her trembling; there seemed no place for me. I felt that I did not care for the means by which this woman's mind had been broken, but I was relieved when I was no longer with her. This was deplorable, but the fact remained. There had been a number of factors and their effect had been cumulative. At first the troops had welcomed me – the sincerity of their welcome had been difficult to assess: it had been largely artificial, but they had had to be certain of my loyalty. I had proved that I could be trusted, but they had kept me outside, and so I had become isolated. This had made for a double action. The mutual dislike had increased. Then there had been a horrible incident. They had held up a car and robbed the passengers; the driver had been taken out and shot. And I had discovered the fun in such business.

# Chapter 3

I KNEW WHERE TO FIND the person I was looking for. After scrambling up the path, I arrived at
the building and was asked to wait by a young girl
in grey uniform. She explained that she would leave
me with him. As she left, he gazed after her. I found
at first that I could not talk to him in any language
that he knew. "So, you live here," I said. He was not
at ease. I smiled at him, said his daughter had told
me about him. He led me into a small room. I was
seated on a red plush couch and he sat on my right
in a red plush armchair. Before us was a round table.
Two small windows facing me lit the room. Outside I
could hear animals bumping and rubbing themselves
against the walls of the house. "Am I to be allowed to
visit her?" I asked. "No." "Does she live openly? Does
she still use the same name?" "Yes." "Tell me, what
is her position?" "She is safe. While she continues to
work for us, she will be protected; no matter where
she may be taken, don't worry – we will not lose sight
of her." He got up. "I must offer you hospitality." He
left the room to return carrying a bottle of wine. "It is
home-made wine." Chains hung round his thick neck,
rested on his heavy body. We sipped the wine. We con-
versed. The sun cut sharply into the room. He smiled.
He tried to entice me. I refused. I was aware of the
animals moving around. He told me he was head of
the family. In a burst of energy he shouted that she

was his child; his family must not die out. Out of his wallet came photographs of the girl. My interest was qualified by hesitation and reserve. I noted the great variety; her talent for adaptation; her wide range of mood, which was not at first apparent. He showed me another and another, without being aware of the differences – the backward slope, the white skin, the canopied eye, the arm: slender and colourless. They could have been different people. She expressed a jumbling of use and fancy. In one she came running through a doorway, the stones of her necklace swinging above her upper lip; in another, younger, she covered her fingers in long grass. There were none above a certain age. I asked him, in a calm, uninterested tone, when she had left home. "She said she would leave. She came towards me to kiss me. I seized a chair. I had a bad temper. I meant no harm. I had always admired her." He held a photo of his wife, but he did not show it to me. He said it was a poor likeness – the others had been taken from him; he had stolen this one. "I'm sorry," he apologized: he had knocked the table and spilt the wine. "I don't seem to be able to manage this." With his handkerchief he mopped up the wine from the table and from the floor at my feet, wiping off a few drops that had fallen on my shoes. "I am getting old, though my nerves are still good; I sleep soundly. As long as I can keep going and complete the work." "You still work?" "I am a worker." "But what exactly does that mean?" He looked slightly embarrassed. "I obtain meat, and the town buys it. More or less." "I see. Is that all?" "More or less." He had tried, clumsily, to avoid my question. It was too hot. I was getting drunk. I opened the window. I could see the outside of the wooden building – a large hall was set behind the main part of the house and screened from the road by trees. The commander's armoured car drove slowly past. "I had to buy meat. Everything was wrecked." "Where did you get the meat from?" "The countryside. It came by lorry." I smiled at him and got up from my chair. He said quickly: "I shall tell you everything, the bad as well as the good. What do you want to know?" I knew this game – I had played it with both sides – the more open-handed the host appeared, the more he had to hide. He held out his hand to me and led me into a long, low room containing tables; we walked down the narrow corridor between the tables, past a notice for "Silence", readers intent on newspapers – forty readers to a table. I tried to make out the foreign titles of the papers. He took my arm. "There's nothing here – we'll go into the schoolroom and you'll know where you are." My glance returned to the page. "Do you not want to go?" "I'm in no hurry; I'll come soon." Four young men got up from one of the tables and came smiling and mumbling towards me; I found myself nudged and bundled towards the door. "Where are we going?" More and more of them followed me into the next room, and before I could quite tell how I had got there, I heard the door shut behind me. A young soldier was teaching arithmetic to a class of about fifty older men: they were learning Roman numerals; each in turn went to the blackboard to write a date in Roman figures. The teacher asked: "What was the date of the great battle?" Came a prompt reply from the massed troops. Questions and answers about the battle occupied a few minutes; the writing of the date was a matter of seconds, and then on to the next historical date. No doubt it was a lesson in arithmetic, but to a casual observer it seemed to consist mostly of history. The class by their replies showed that they had a remarkable knowledge of recent history. The young teacher told me that only combatants were taught history – the difference between their education and that of others was that they were made to realize the importance of history. I said that this could mean anything. The teaching of history depended on the teacher. One would explain events as he saw them, another would teach otherwise. "Oh yes." I asked him whether he himself received instruction on methods or approach. "I teach as I please. But mine is a unique position. It was my father's intention that it should be so."

While the father had been uniformed – with medals, buttons, epaulettes, a ring on his forefinger, a tough old man – his son was of another type: he had a gloomy smile, a subdued expression, which marked a face not yet crushed, a moral agnosticism different from anything I had seen. Yet the only blood was the blood of the father; the son had to fight him with the hope of a wild animal, with a cold, bare silence which could not be beaten, with an obedience which accused. While he taught, the son was on his own: "In the occupied areas the population slowly but steadily decreases, while in the liberated territories it as inevitably expands." He pointed to a map – a large space containing gold, enclosed by forts, squares of black. In moments of seriousness, in the tone of his voice and the words used, there was always the same line – a pathway to the dead. He was in pain, but would have no doctor: doctors were "dull and pointless". The revolutionary troops sang songs together with clapping hands and dancing, and the whole point was something of love, with allusions to their life in the town. "My father objects to the dancing, though dancing is our only amusement. He has a conviction that nothing can be clean."

When he looked past his father towards me, the expected cold was felt – the air was as if it had passed over ice. He was young; he had seen the world, the blue line in the distance; his eyes bold, well shaped, deep blue; startling pieces of ice floated in the blue. Half the face looked straight over the sea; he was tall, not ugly, yet confined and bound, cut by the river itself. The father said his son would not stand the cold, and it was true. He cracked to pieces, was half destroyed – there appeared a break in the old shape; he faced me, taller and thinner. This deterioration was to be observed. Rouge was used, his cheeks painted to imitate youth, his origin lost as it stretched out, his neck the beak of a duck. In the shadow of his father he failed. He was no longer remarkable. The absence of concentration – it was the first time I had noticed it. I had never known a father who killed. He continued to teach the history of the party, and of his father's role: "Full of courage he assumed power. He destroyed the organization and divided the party." His father stood at the back of the crowded room. He nodded to his son, who went with him to the adjoining room; the son's voice, higher-pitched than the older man's, could be heard through the board partition. "I am tired and would like to go to bed. When the sun rose, I was so tired that I could not enjoy anything. The rush of water coming over showed itself; I would not make the colours so rich; twenty feet of water rushed over in a column."

The white beds and the delicate white curtains – no flowers, no books, no work but mental death. The faces were happy. The lack of hope brought calm. The windows were never opened. The rules, dress, system of life, were those of the army. Side by side with the doctor stalked the father with all the knowledge. I noticed the names – some familiar, some foreign – written over the beds. I was a man who had been sent to study documents, yet they did not accuse me of indifference. The punishments were the same as in the army. They were denied the little food, made to kneel, allowed to talk only in echoes. The father visited the dying, gave them water, touched their foreheads and noted them down in the records, which they did not see. The son remembered and spoke of his death, which he did not know of. He saw a shabby monument which marked the spot. The land belonged to the people. He told me his dream of his death. He was three men. The weather was cold. The three looked small on the battlefield. Straight under the steep rock, coloured brown and yellow, the untidy town, full of colour, was reflected in the water. The season was over, the boats no longer ran, the river fell straight over the cliff; there was no decline; you saw no rocks – they were hidden by water, which rushed with violence – it was not a fall like other falls; it was not what it was – it had been diverted to make electric light. "I did not realize it was my last chance of seeing lights – I saw nothing but small white wreaths for the dead; the trees had been cut down – there were no trees in the place, no gardens; the land not built upon was covered with rubbish. The last man missed his footing and fell. He was already fifty yards away; he threw his arms into the air – the fatal instinct; the body was not recovered, though it may have been. The life was over. Can anything be more logical?" I tried to understand the sequence of events. He was ill, but still seemed to want to know more, spoke with an odd pride, grinned with pleasure when I told him that, though I was a foreigner, I believed that sooner or later some form of victory must come. He let me see then that he knew something of the struggle that was going on. I would not soon forget the intelligent face. He had not spoken of his sister. I asked him to write her a note. He said he was incapable of writing; he could not remember her name; he could not write a single word. It was not writing but real work that was required of him. As soon as he was well, he would ask to be transferred to the fighting front.

In his private room, the father gave me fried eggs and bread. He played the violin. He was drunk. We played cards, each trying to cheat – he distracted me with his talk. "I have seen the destruction of the best men. One wife would not allow her husband to be buried; she gave us the name and his body was sent by car, concealed under my coat, a hat over his face. We told her he had escaped by aeroplane – I remember the streaming from her eyes; he had died defeated, in the corridor, killed. How she suffered. And the lips of some agonized mother I will never know, her son among the missing. He had left that day, before lunch. No return. He had disappeared without reason. Yet I am not worried; I don't feel." I threw my cards down. "I must find the girl. I am not interested in anything else." "First we must eat. You must stay – we'll have a party." He gave me his son's room. Two wooden chairs and a table: the essentials. He pushed open the door without knocking, stood in his military greatcoat; his face had a hard, obstinate look that had not been there before. He sat down opposite me, offered me a cigarette and began a drunken monologue. "My teeth are bad, and so is the life I have to lead." He fell asleep in the chair; I took the lit cigarette from between his fingers. As I had been told that I would not be able to buy any food on my journey, I stole from his cupboard the rest of the bread, some tea and a few eggs. Before I left I noticed with pleasure the trembling of his legs. We were both foreigners.

# Chapter 4

I REJOINED THE REGULAR TROOPS. They talked
of bandits and mass slaughter, but I knew they
were deceiving themselves – it was the new human
mind. I saw signs of recent battles; I noted them
particularly.

The sky was usually grey, yet I could see the road for
miles; every object was distinct: piles of stones, gravel,
a steamroller, axes in use, logs, small bridges. We drove
along red roads, between trees sunk into soaking fields.
We reached the forest, and from then on it was never out
of sight, even from the suburbs of the town, house after
house – people walking, carrying; bundled up human
beings. It was cold; we lost the way; it rained when it
should have been fine.

My reckless driver handled his car – he put on the
brakes to avoid a collision; I was frantic; the powerful
car spun round twice before overturning; I sprang from
the car. He remained calm. The car righted itself; he
gave a contemptuous flap of his hand, indifferent to
my shouted protest. The road was metalled; the earth
had frozen; the forest was not far away; the land was
derelict. "Now we have lost contact with our escort,"
the driver said. "We don't need an escort." "Impossible.
We cannot go on" – with fear in his eyes – "there are
bandits; the roads are too dangerous." "We are going
on." "I have other things to do – important duties – I
cannot go any farther." "You must go on – it is an

order." "No. Stay where you are." I had no alterna-
tive. I depended on him – not least because I could
not drive the car.

"The road is not really so bad." He did not reply.
We were in the front seats of the car, by the side of
the road, just within the forest. He did not say "this
is the forest"; he did not speak – he had other things
on his mind. He studied an instruction booklet, which
seemed to relate to the revolver which he had taken
from its holster and laid across his knees. A farm to
our left had, or had not, a patch of birch trees growing
close to the walls of the farmhouse – I was not certain
about it. A family was being taken from the house and
loaded onto a lorry, together with their belongings.
The driver noticed my concern. "Do you want to see
them taken away? It's only half a mile." "What is there
to see?" "Nothing. It's just a place like this." He said
that to intrigue me, to interest me in something else.
I replied: "Then there is no point in wasting time over
it." The map he showed me, on which was marked the
place to which the people were to be taken, showed
clearly that to have followed them would have taken
me in the wrong direction, back towards the troops'
headquarters. I could see also that his map did not
correspond with the map I had made – nor did it bear
any relation to the map the girl had given me. "By the
way," I asked him, "will the family be loaded from
one lorry onto another? Or will they stay on the same
lorry?" "They change at a small town thirty miles away;
I hear that they are going to be allowed to stay in that
place. It is a pity there is no road to it – you ought to
see it: it's a beautiful town." "I'm afraid there is not

enough daylight left." "You should see it. The fountains are famous." "Wasn't the town destroyed?" "No, the inhabitants were cleared out and it was preserved for hunting. The army was sent round it, not through it, so it did not suffer. It still contains rare specimens of wild animals." He showed me a newspaper photograph of a young man in a light-grey uniform similar to his own, though his was darker. He laughed. "A boy. A bandit killed in a raid; he was thirteen years old." I said that this was a surprise to me – I had not realized that these gangsters were so young. "Are there many left?" I asked.

"Perhaps eight or ten. Far too many – they must be shot down." I was winning his confidence. He talked seriously, with terrific enthusiasm. "They are a pest. Their stupidities and brutalities no longer trouble us, but they attack farms and kill the animals. They drink the blood and leave the carcasses." "Blood?" "They get desperate and kill sheep. They had all been driven back across the frontier, until one of their old leaders escaped from prison and built them up again." He showed me another photograph, of a naked man crawling between ranks of soldiers like a dog – a small, tough dog roaming the ruins. "We have a battalion competition," he said. "There is a money prize for any man who can capture two bandits on the same day. This one was caught in a pit. A hole was dug, the top covered, mud and grass scattered over it. We left some food – he was starving and made a rush for it. The earth collapsed under him. It was cruel. Imagine the weight: the earth fell on top of him as he crashed down." His face was sweating with excitement;

I had a sudden glimpse of what it must have been like. "We pulled him out the next day – he was alive, but with badly broken limbs; we chased him, you can see, hemmed him in; after I managed to get a rope round his legs he couldn't resist; once the noose was pulled tightly we dragged him in the desired direction. The others struggled to get their ropes round him – they leant on him with all their weight; even that was not the end of it." "You seem to have enjoyed yourselves." He pulled back the sleeve of his shirt. His upper arm was contained in a plaster cast; his finger went along the surface of the stuff, which cut his arm almost into equal parts. He wanted to talk freely. I knew that the way to get him to tell me what had become of the girl was to ask him about himself. He told me about his family, the war, and, in a gesture of friendship, he said that I must sign his autograph book. "You must start a fresh page." "I am in a special category," I remarked, as I wrote my name on a blank page at the back of the instruction booklet. As I wrote, I lifted the corner of the preceding page, to try to read the other names. He snatched the book away. "Tell me," I asked in a friendly tone, "how were you taken into the army?" "When I got to the camp I was told what would happen if I didn't join up – they told us again and again. Then the war ended and they said we were no longer required – that we could return home. I refused. They sent me away. I picked up some food from the floor and was sent to prison for stealing." "When did you learn that you were wanted again?" "They never told me, but I knew it would happen, and I started off. The nearest railway station was two hundred miles away; I walked from one place to the other." "How did you manage to live?" "I did some work, serving my country, then went on." He was under twenty. He had an amused look on his face. "I was joking," he said. "I was not taken – I went by myself." "You must have been taken," I protested. "I am telling the truth." "Did you have to prove who you were before they would take you back?" He laughed. "No, they knew."

While waiting in the car, we had eaten the remains of our food. It was still light: I could still see the trees; I wanted to see them. I said to him: "You know that I am trying to trace a girl. Have you any information as to where she may be?" "She's in a room." He was joking. I would get nothing from him. I needed to speak to her. I was exhausted and lay on the ground – it was frozen; there was no light or water; she lived in a destroyed town; she could only hope to get one kind of work. The bridges were down, nothing would be done; it was impossible – there was no point in looking for the girl: the town was erased, nothing remained, she had been killed, people lived in holes, nothing lived above the ground.

The lorry returned, filled with soldiers armed with sub-machine guns. The commander was in civilian clothes. He had heard of my change in plans, and he made it clear that he and his men would accompany me. "I have come to offer you an escort for your journey." "That is most thoughtful of you," I replied, "but there is no need for me to take advantage of your generosity. I came this far without an escort, and I think I can manage the rest alone." "Then I shall follow you." "In that case I shall be delighted to have your company. I shall be leaving immediately." We shook hands, and he walked back to the lorry. My driver mumbled: "I don't like it. That's bad." He studied his map: "Don't you think it would be better if we went through the forest tomorrow rather than tonight?" I agreed. I had had enough. I told him to inform the commander. "From now on he must be advised of my plans or change of plans." We could not take the route by which we had come. The temporary wooden bridge had been swept away by the spring floods.

White clouds and sunlight: the winter had gone. Spring revealed the tears in our clothes. The troops put up a prefabricated shed. The length of the pieces varied, but the thickness was five inches by five inches, tongued on one side, grooved on the opposite edge – one piece slotted into the other. The commander shouted orders: "We need twelve hundred blocks to build a house. Work with fury. March. March. A town can be built in this way." It was for my benefit. They cemented the floor and the walls; the long process ended, the floor soon spoilt – the whitened stone got coated with mud. I asked why they were building a house so isolated in the forest. They blew up the house and burned the greater part of the two remaining walls. Under the open sky they assembled the planks and wooden frames to construct the wooden shed which was to serve as a temporary shelter until the house could be rebuilt in a proper manner, and they slung petrol over the wood and fired bullets into the pile.

It was near the end of the steady, plodding slaughter. They were shooting from the upper storeys of gutted houses; they hurled down bricks; bricks blocked the streets.

By myself, without a guide, I didn't know where to go next; I wondered how she was earning her living. It looked like being a filthy business. I was tired of trying to keep warm, tired of the tedious task of rebuilding. "When do we return?" No answer.

The escort was ready. We drove at seventy miles an hour. We were in control, flying from town to town. The people were aware of our presence: they went about in threes; they whispered as we passed; when we were close they preferred not to speak – it was too risky. We passed an openwork stone wall. "What is that?" "Our monument to the men who died fighting." "How many men?" "Eight." "How did they die?" "They were tried and shot." From their precious supply of petrol they gave us enough for the journey back to town. There were not many hours of daylight left. The driver mumbled: "I think the light will last. We shall make it." He tried, furiously. One hour's light still in hand, a bare arm stopped the car; the door opened; he had half clambered in when he cried "Who is in there?" and fell back onto the road. The driver went to him but returned alone. Ahead was a cart loaded with hay; it kept to the middle of the road in spite of our violent hooting; we fired shots in the air and it still kept to the middle of the road; the cart had a front axle and a rear axle; the rebel farmer was a careful driver; we were hundreds of miles from the town painted on the back of the cart. The road was bad – anything might be in store for us.

We forced the cart into the ditch at the side of the road; the horse, tangled with the harness, lay on its back in the ditch – the hoofs in the air reminded me of a scene in a film. We heard the man calling out; we found the body gleaming yellow; he wiped the tears from his face, rushed forwards and demanded, was silent when the driver told him, then went over to look at the body and walked on towards the village. A couple of men walked about the village; no effort had been made to repair the doors of the houses. "It is difficult to get anyone interested. They have no civic pride," the commander informed me. "They are not progressive – they have a school but not one student. The hens lay small eggs and the hogs don't fatten. What can we do? They are like insects; they store small things they have made; they have gold hidden in the earth or under the roof. It's been a bad season – they have become victims and left their houses, or they have stayed inside and starved. They need money – only money would protect them against the bandits and the havoc that follows the spring floods. The forests could have been exploited, the railways put in order; three hundred-ton barges could have sailed up that river and passed below the bridge."

We tore through the town. We wrecked like fury. The public baths had been only partly destroyed – they had begun to repair the doors. "We have a powerful new light – it was installed the other day – and we have painted the doors." We wrenched the handles off the doors, shot to pieces the apparatus, slit the padding in the soundproof room. We crowded into the room. We ate bread and ham. "What do you want?" Silence. A boy in a light-grey jacket with a sub-machine gun:

"Get out or I shoot." He stared round at us, his fear shown by his grip on the butt; he was trying to work out what to do next. "We'll never give up. We'll fight. We don't need tractors – we want horses, we want bread." Some drunken soldiers had shot one of the horses. The commander spoke quietly: "Look at this." He took a wrapped toffee from his pocket and threw it on the floor a couple of feet in front of the boy. The young soldier, awkwardly, transferring the heavy gun from his right hand to his left, bent forwards to pick up the sweet. A shot sounded but made no echo in the soundproof room. The commander continued: "As for horses, only the collective has the right to own them; if one or a dozen horses die, the individual has no cause to fear."

We had breakfast of white rolls and butter, two eggs and coffee. I was accustomed to destruction – there were standards of destruction – the little town had been destroyed. There was nothing. The thing had disappeared. Not a brick visible. A man appeared out of the ground, a boy from a hole stood beside the man. "What do you live on?" "Potatoes." "No corn?" "I can plant only potatoes." The commander indicated that things were not so bad now that the land had been cleared of mines: animals were no longer injured by exploding shells. "Not long ago any one of these people would have lost his own son or his wife in exchange for a sound calf or a pig." He had seen cattle caught in minefields – whole collections of the feet of animals, legs severed at the knee, bones sprouting from bushes; and, in cottages, collections of hoofs, fossilized, kept.

I changed my plans. I told the commander that I intended to stop at the next large town. "As you please." Racing through the rain, the driver accelerated, the heavy tyres skidded sideways across the metalled road. I looked back. "Where is the escort?" He seemed indifferent, increased his speed; the rain smashed against the windscreen. "Stop. We must wait for them." They soon discovered their mistake, and a minute or two later we saw them behind us, as I intended. We drove on towards the town — a few lights miles ahead across the bare land uninterrupted by any tree or building — no traffic, no noise; we travelled slowly. Under waiting clouds we entered the darkened town. The headlights of the lorries flashed on blank spaces — remains of houses, flat ground where shops had stood. "You won't be able to go any farther." I got out and walked towards the seven-storeyed silent blaze from the lit windows of the new hotel. Behind me the driver worked in the rain, mending a punctured tyre.

# Chapter 5

LOOKING ACROSS THE TOWN from the marble steps of the hotel, if I did not lift my eyes beyond the ground floor, I could believe I was at home, in the shopping centre of a normal town, but above the ground floor there was nothing. The upper windows had nested snipers, the walls around them had been smashed by shells. The hotel was empty, half-built: it had electricity but no carpets, no glass to the windows. The few undamaged houses were used as barracks – more than five thousand troops garrisoned the town, but they were kept apart, and were often difficult to find. One large old building near the town centre was reserved for officers, the ground floor used as a restaurant, the upper floors for private parties.

Though I knew the answer to the question, I asked the commander whether anyone lived in the rooms upstairs. He said that the rooms were occupied from time to time. From my seat in the car I could see curtains in one of the upper windows. It was her room. I said I was hungry and asked the commander to take me into the restaurant. "The food is poor," he replied. "The whole house is badly built. The foundations are shifting; only the ground floor is habitable. The central heating does not work properly – it is always cold and depressing." He clutched the top of the seat of the car alongside me. I was alone with a fanatic. He tried to get me into an argument, but it was futile – I was ready for him. I kept quiet. I had the information I needed. It was only my need of his help to get into the heavily guarded building that caused me to remain polite to him.

Two soldiers waited for permission to speak to the commander. They were talking together; there was a laugh, and it had something sly in it. The commander said to me suddenly: "I presume it is still your intention to help us obtain medical supplies?" I answered vaguely: "I'm sorry, it was not possible—" He interrupted: "You were followed. Our information is that the person you visited is in no position to assist us." I said nothing. "You led us to him. Although he had fled before, we were able to check with certainty his identity and role, we were able to learn something from the documents left behind – among them photographs of the girl in whom you show such interest." I replied: "She can't help you. Why do you continue to suspect her?" He held the car door open, but prevented me from getting out. "We have to be careful. She is confused; she has a natural reluctance to discuss her father's whereabouts, but we are confident that a period of re-education will change her attitude. It would be in your interests to persuade her to cooperate." I looked at my watch: it was five o'clock. I made no comment. I had not changed my plans. "The driver needs food," I said. "He cannot leave the car unattended." "We can provide an armed guard for the car." The commander smiled and went up the steps into the building.

I got out of the car and spoke to a child who was sitting on the steps. "How old are you?" "Eight." "Who lives in that big house?" She would not speak again – she had seen the armoured car.

The commander reappeared at the top of the steps with two armed soldiers. He beckoned me up. When I reached him, he took a sheet of paper from his pocket and handed it to me. It was a list of names. I said simply: "There are hundreds of names here." He replied: "Very few. Practically none." "But that is impossible." "We have had dreadful losses." He spoke hurriedly as he took me past the guards, through the crowded restaurant, swing doors, kitchens, up two flights of stairs. "Now I tell you. I cannot tell you. It is nothing new." He ran up the stairs ahead of me, laughing in an unexpected way. His military training and his supple leather boots made this kind of game easier for him than for me. Outside a newly painted door he stopped and waited. He took the list from my hand. I said: "These names mean nothing to me." The door was not opened. Then it was slightly opened. Fear and pleasure in half a face: "Why bring him here?"

A table. A floor. We faced each other under the glare of the light. Her body rigid, she faced us. We waited. "You work together," she said defiantly. "Nonsense." She persisted: "He knew what I had said to you." The commander moved towards her: "Let's talk about something more cheerful – about the old days." He dominated. We had met, but we had met in a fog. Troops marched in the streets; she heard them below; her hand went to the light. She hesitated. The commander took off his spectacles and wiped the dust from them; his eyes were dark blurs. She swiftly looked towards me and managed to convey that she could not speak now. I stared at her. She seemed to shiver. I would have to wait. I asked the commander: "Has she all the things she needs?" He seemed to realize that he had missed something, and answered irritably: "They are on their way." I had had similar replies before. I said: "Excellent. When precisely may they be expected to arrive?" There was a silence. He said: "Some parcels have been delayed. Your people at a meeting prevented them from being sent." "So that is the story." "It is true." I looked round the room: a long gilt mirror, a lamp, two herrings, a pair of stockings over the sink. "What is her attitude generally?" I asked. "She will not cooperate. She was asked her father's name; she gave her mother's maiden name."

A kind of sunlight shone into the room – blue without any trace of red in it – so blue as to be harsh. I knew I would get nothing done. I left the room and waited in the corridor. I heard him ask her: "Where is your father?" "I don't know." "And your mother?" "She is at home, ill." "A lie. Why are you not working?" "I am not allowed to work." "How many are there at home?" "The baby and my brother." "How old is your brother?" "Thirteen." "What does he do?" "He carries water." "Has he a work permit?" "He does not get paid – only tips; it is no life here – he wants to go to America: he would get tips besides his wages…"

I walked down the corridor; it was full of dust and rubbish – the floor had not been cleaned. In the restaurant I sat at the long table; it was crowded; as I sat down they stopped their conversation to watch me. I walked over to the window and looked out. They lost interest in me and continued talking in low tones. "Things are getting worse." "He did not come home." "His wife has gone to look for him – she has not yet returned." They were everywhere – I could hear nothing but their insistent conversations.

I moved towards the door. The driver stopped me and told me in the friendliest way that I had "taken the wrong road". With a grin he showed me what he called his "old autograph book". My name had been carefully inked out. He closed the book. I knew my luck had come to an end. I tried to regain his friendship – I asked him where his next job would take him. He said he was driving north to search for some pieces of machinery – he had already located some crates, thanks to information given him by a workman who had assisted in the packing. I said I was sorry I had not the time to get from him more details of what would normally have interested me as a commercial operation. I asked him how he acquired machinery and got it transported without cash or credit. "Well, the bits and pieces arrive." "Who pays the workmen for setting them up?" "They get paid cash for work done." I could see that he would not disclose more than this.

I joined a group of young officers; I got them to talk. They had no suspicions – they thought they were telling me secrets, though they knew nothing – they had no idea of the work being done – I could not hint at what I knew. Even here I heard her father's name – the name that was disturbing the country. In this garrison town, his friends had gathered others who shared his views. I thought of the girl in the room: she was sitting on the bed; she had guessed something. I felt I had left her a mile behind.

The crowd packed itself tightly round me; I heard the commander mutter to the driver: "This fellow is a foreigner – get more out of him for his fare." "No use: he asked the price before starting." The crowd split into two, leaving a corridor along which the commander walked; he called me to come with him. He went to his chair at the head of the table. I was given, as a place of honour, the seat next to his. My elevated position soon became one of isolation. The rest of the company began to ignore my presence. The commander did not speak to me. For some time, I was not able to order a meal, and when I tried to find out what I could get to eat the host became rather embarrassed. It was evident that there was not enough food for such a large party. He did not wish to abandon the banquet; he imagined it was an event in his life. From what I could gather, he insisted that he could provide us with veal cutlets, but naturally it would take time for the meal to be prepared. I could hear the commander making polite conversation to people opposite and on either side of me, but he did not mention or speak to me.

Someone came in from the street and made some kind of signal to the commander. He came up and stood between us. There was a quiet but agitated discussion. The commander turned to me: "There has been a mistake. This man and his wife were expecting me to have dinner with them, and everything is prepared. But I have, as you see, ordered dinner here and I cannot cancel it. What should I do?" It was seven thirty in the evening; there was still an hour's daylight and dusk. "We can have a hurried meal here," I said, "and then go on to the other house for dinner." He looked surprised, but made no comment. I seemed to have created a bad impression. I had assumed that I was included in the invitation, but from the way in which the stranger looked at me it appeared that I was mistaken. I decided that it would merely magnify the error if I were to make any kind of explanation or apology. "There is nothing to be done," the commander said at last. I sensed the unspoken protest. He refused the invitation to dinner.

To make matters worse, we had nearly an hour to wait before the cutlets arrived. The food was almost uneatable. The meat and soup were served together: the meat was overcooked; the soup tasted sweet, like ink.

I was relegated to my aloof place of honour as the rest settled down to their food. Now and again I caught odd scraps of conversation. Once the subject was myself, who, it appeared, had had the audacity to go into the town on market day in an attempt to meet people from the surrounding countryside. But "they trust the police", one of them said, and, turning to me: "Nothing you can say will alter their opinions. If you try to find things out, they will say they know nothing."

Silence descended on the company as a second huge dish of cutlets was placed on the table. The commander spoke to me: "I advise you to pack up the remains of the food. You never know when you will get your next meal, or you may know someone who would enjoy the scraps." I noticed that he hardly touched the food. Encouraged by his new friendliness, I asked him his opinion of the girl, and I was surprised to discover that he was quite willing to talk about her: "She is no more brutal than the rest; she is not wilfully cruel. Only by practical experiment can the truth be learnt: before condemning her, take her place – pay her that compliment." "She has no energy," I said cautiously. "She seems to be thinking of something else most of the time." "She needs more intelligent training," he replied. "A hand laid on her side would have been enough – there should have been no need to rely on the sudden pain of the whip. Enough for the hand to have been raised as if to strike, though in moments of excitement—" Through the windows I could see the river. I was suffering from a curious sort of fever, as if I inhabited another body. He continued talking quietly to me: "These bandits are becoming a problem. They are tough – otherwise they would not be alive. They have lost the habits of civilized life. These filthy people are driving us out of this decent town which we have made. They are a lower order of human beings: they are not like the ordinary, decent individual – they are not willing to obey orders, so their decency is gone." "They need care." "I'll give them care. I shall examine them all. If I find one case of disease, I shall destroy every one of them. It will be in the national interest; I shall make them see that. I will talk to their representatives." "Representatives?"

"Worms. I shall convince them. I shall arrange joint control to avoid delays. It is grand work. It is full of difficulties, but we shall get over them. Were you able to talk to the girl alone? Did you discuss our policies?" "She was told 'no work, no food'." "She should have come to me." "Your clerk told her that you were busy and that she was to return in the afternoon." "Sheer incompetence. I shall be ruthless." "When she arrived in the town, she went without food or water for twenty-four hours." "I am investigating that." He dashed across the room and picked up a telephone receiver. "What is the latest news you can give me about the progress of the investigations?" The girl at the central telephone exchange did not know the part she was meant to play. He slammed down the receiver. "They are following the matter up. We are going to stamp it out. Any bandit found escaping over the frontier is to be brought before the court, dragged in front of a judge. He is to be tried by special tribunal. The minimum sentence is ten years." I said that she had no wish to escape – she planned to settle in the district. He replied: "Do you happen to know whether she intends to settle here because of the climate, or is she merely trying to get as near the frontier as possible?" "She would like to buy a shop and remain." "I shall help her. Not only has she suffered terribly, she is also a most valuable asset to the state. You must see her again once more before you go." He wrote out an order for me to be allowed to visit her. The order was in the form of a travel permit; we were to be taken together to a certain destination – the name of the town was then unknown. I understood what had happened – what arrangements had been made – while I had been entertained with food and friendly conversation.

# Chapter 6

W E DROVE THROUGH the sunset, over miles of new roads, towards a chain of hills in red stone, through stone quarries which provided the stone for the great stadium, the modern hospital, for constructing the aerodrome. Ruins, alternately red and grey, were splashed with red – the red grew from inside the ruins. Without moving, the earth shaped; the red persisted as we drove: at dusk a crown of domed red blown away into water; red arches opened straight onto water on either side.

All morning we drove slowly; I was thirsty – there was no water. We stopped; we had an excellent meal, seven or eight courses – I should have liked to stay, but the car was waiting.

A coat was thrown over her. She stared stupidly. No one spoke. No one told her where she was being taken. I leant forwards to ask the driver. He nodded. "We're almost there." With a quick movement he inserted a rod between her legs; her strength drained away.

Surrounded by wide grounds, by a high wall, I stayed silent. I heard a faint jangling from the bracelets she wore on her wrists. Doors were unlocked and locked; she walked forwards, dragging the rings with her down the corridor, through doors which were unlocked and locked, down the continuing corridor, each door noisily slammed behind her. She touched the rings. Then she forgot them. They were no longer important. If there had been others willing to take her, none of this would have happened.

From the outside the main building had the appearance of a mansion: marble pillars, ornate gilt, complex decorations. The building, though dilapidated, was not in ruins; the upper floors were kept from crushing the lower by steel struts placed upright and threaded into the walls of the corridors and rooms. A wooden barrier, topped by a low steel rail, extended the length of the entrance hall, separating a crowd of women and children from the administration. Here parents searched for their children, children for their parents. I enquired about her and was told that she had been asking for news of me. Her block number indicated that she was in the central block.

In the courtyard through which I walked to reach the central block, two girls in protective clothing, wearing masks, were examining the contents extracted from the pockets of the dead. If positive identification resulted, the news was passed to those waiting, and the contents of the pockets given to the nearest relative.

The central block composed forty rooms, each with a grated hole as a window. It was the store that interested me – a cupboard crammed with clothes, medicines, soap and food. The heavy sliding doors to each room had been pushed back, and I had the impression that the occupants had retreated to the wall farthest from the door and in each case were crouched under the window round a small iron stove. One room was empty except for a table covered with a brown sheet; a stretcher blocked the corridor outside – we stepped over it, and walked on down the wide corridor with rooms opening on either side, the commander first, then myself, the driver trotting behind. In spite of the open doors, there was not enough air. The commander said that normally the double doors were kept closed.

I wanted to see the girl at once, but the commander insisted that I talk to the people in the rooms, implying that they would be disappointed if I walked by without greeting them. He stood back, and allowed the driver to assume the part of a guide: "Each room contains two families." In five rooms I counted maybe thirty women and children, with perhaps two or three men. I asked where the people slept. "They have bundles of clothes. They sleep on them. Those who have nothing sleep on boards."

They squatted silently, keeping back from the heavy doors; only the children crept closer, peering curiously at us. I spoke to one of the women crouched at the other end of the room. She shouted back in a harsh, unpleasant voice: "They took them. They sent them back." "What do you mean?" "My husband and my two children." "Where are they now?" "They sent them back." She would not come nearer. I asked one of the children who had poked her head round the door and was looking down the corridor whether she went to school. "We work in the factory, making bricks." "Do you get paid?" She shook her head. The commander said curtly: "They had time to find normal work." A boy pushed through the crowd of women and came up to me. I thought I remembered him – he resembled the boy with the sub-machine gun. He made me feel his ragged grey jacket. "I cannot get more because it is written on my identity card – one jacket, one pullover, one pair of shoes – and nothing is said about them being old clothes." I was wearing a new suit of greenish-yellow tweed and my heavy overcoat. The commander had on his fur-lined waterproof and military boots. There was nothing I could say. I was wasting my time, I knew that. I was not thinking clearly – I was not asking the right questions, nor taking proper note of the answers. The commander had given me a bar of chocolate; I broke off two squares and offered them to the boy. "Why don't we get new things?" the boy asked. The driver interrupted him: "I work. Why don't you work? No work, no clothes." The women came forwards and pressed round us: "They won't give us food. If we can't eat, we can't work." My guide repeated: "Those who won't work shall not eat." "They won't let us work." "That's a lie. I'll get you work," the commander shouted back at them, and, bending his head close to mine, said quietly: "If you wish to see her tonight, we should leave now."

"They treat us like bandits." The crowd followed us down the corridor. "We fought. They disarmed us. We worked in the forests. Those who were ill were left to die. They deported us, then took us back and jailed us – now they call us bandits. They won't give us work; they won't give us food." The driver took a whistle from his pocket and blew several sharp blasts. Guards came thundering down the corridor. The prisoners' lives were spent in terror; they rushed back into their rooms, they tried to close the sliding doors, but the locks were electrically controlled; the children banged tins, they threw stones into the corridor. The guards forced their way into the rooms – four guards to a room – the doors slid shut behind them.

We were in normal surroundings. We walked along grated steel floors to the dining hall. The commander had tickets which gave the number of our table. Small tables were set along three walls, leaving the centre clear for dancing. At the far end a jazz band played. The driver sat alone at the next table. There were few women – the place was full of thick-necked businessmen. "They made their money," the commander explained, "and they like to spend it. They don't have to tell me where they got their money from." It was incongruous, in that room, where each piece of furniture spoke of former owners. We talked of difficulties, lack of this, lack of that. Food was scarce – food was a constant theme. He would not say much about his work. "Large packages – they send us the dead, discs, portraits, paper soaked in blood. We are obliged to sort them, handling each object with care, repacking and redirecting sealed boxes in thousands."

I asked him which room had been used for the children. He said: "This room." He described the six hundred children packed into the darkened room; the marks of their fingers could be seen on the walls. "They must have known what was to happen." "We told them it was to be a concert – we provided music, from a violin and a piano, until a woman stepped in front of the curtain and called for silence."

I was being diverted from my object. I asked him directly: "When may I speak to the girl?" "You may see her. A meeting has been arranged." "Where is she now?" "In my room." He paused and added pointedly: "She is resting." I was holding a glass of wine to my mouth: I felt my hand tremble to the point of insanity; I dropped the glass onto the table – it smashed and sent the wine over the cloth. He said calmly: "I took you for a friend. I see I was mistaken." I had begun to apologize, but before I could say more than a few words, he left the table and, after speaking to the driver for a moment, went out of the room. The driver came over to me with a super- cilious smile: "I am asked to inform you that the question of the permit to visit a person charged with a crime against the state can only be dealt with through official channels." "What does that mean?" "You'll have to apply through the office like everyone else."

After I had waited an hour in the outer office, the com- mander came in, but did not appear to notice me. He whispered something to a secretary, and they left the room together. Within a few moments she returned carrying a length of dress material. While she was handling the material and draping it about herself, she turned to me and said irritably: "There's no point in you waiting here." But she merely glanced at me in an impersonal way when I walked past her into the private office.

The commander was alone in his office, with books – a man with a history, his head square and large in bone, his coat black or brown, his well-made boots climbing a steep slope of work. Steel blinds protected his head from the sun; he was aware of the threats which shadowed his life. He got up from his chair and shook hands formally. "You have come at an awkward time," he said. "I received orders to bring you here and answer your questions. I obeyed. That is all." He had an easy manner. I was an official guest. I was offered a seat, but declined it. "I regret I cannot receive you in our senate room, but it is undergoing repair after damage during the war. In what way can I be of service to you?" He looked beyond me at the charts on the walls. I was not deceived. I said: "I don't wish to cause any trouble. I want things to go on as they are; I want to keep the wheels turning." He made a sign, picked up his coat, which had lain neatly across the back of his chair, and walked towards the door. I respected him. I stood aside. He passed close to me. I felt his breath on my face. The light was terribly bright. I watched his face – his mouth moved: "A mistake may have been made." I tried to touch his hand. I asked: "Why do you speak in this way?" His expression changed. "I will make further enquiries. Should I receive a favourable report, arrangements will be made for the transfer of population. In any event, I shall show you everything – the bad as well as the good. And afterwards perhaps you will not be so anxious to see her." He waited for me to go. "I hope she will be released." "She will get out, but only to some other place."

# Chapter 7

I CHANGED MY LIFE. I went among the prisoners taken to the camp for labour purposes. I wanted to make certain; I wanted to get inside; I knew the language. I wanted to learn more, suddenly. Where I might not have understood two words, I got used to their slang and abbreviations. My work was in that place. I began to study murder. I made plans. A few feet between us, the open country beyond. Success depended on whether I could reach the open country afterwards. I studied maps. The plan was complicated: there were roads to be watched; speed was essential; there were two main roads leading to the town – they formed a junction a mile north of the camp.

I watched the driver – his hair was white – he was my man. All the rest were prisoners – he was not. The others wrote to their families – he did not. I examined the identity of this man, I lived with him. He talked – he had no suspicions: he talked about his family, he discussed his girl, showed me her photograph; there was little I did not know about him. He was very particular about his food – he spent hours planning meals – he had trained to be a cook. "I got work which entitled me to a room with furniture, and then I sold the furniture. I bought these trousers and a fur-lined coat. That's how I got this job. I looked the part."

I was no longer myself, but him. I wore his best black trousers; I squeezed into his coat. I could not bring my arms to my sides; my head was too large for the cap; it was hot; the sun hit my head; I was not good-looking enough. I met the commander walking along – I never showed my face; he did not know I had passed. I noted the shape of the commander's thin fingers, felt the texture of his palm. His palm smelt of sweet gas. I knew the time for his death. He was to follow those who had disappeared at his word. I was the person in the crowded courtyard who knew the date of his death. I did not tell him anything. I often walked close to him with my gun; there would have been time – he was in easy range. This time he was larger, bolder, more conspicuous – I happened to catch sight of him crossing the road; I had a clear view of the small person, a fleeting glimpse – he was a tremendously fast walker: always in a hurry, he preferred the open roads to the densely crowded courtyard; he was most careful where he walked.

I did not know that I was being watched. I was stopped by police; a bomb had been thrown. The police closed in. Their caps made them taller; guns on either side; their hands held sticks. I was knocked down by a sergeant of police, my arm crushed by his boots against the wall. He ordered me out of the camp within one hour. A lorry was leaving in forty minutes.

I gave up my plan. I needed to know him better. I threw away my loaded gun – the barrel was hot; it was painful to touch the metal. Then came shots. The pain from my arm underlined the reality of what was happening. The sound of the clump of metal on the floor – a man without legs, false legs and metal feet, carried on a wooden board; I heard a clatter, the driver lit his pipe, he fell dead; I could not prevent the blunder – he was hit by five bullets. The driver, not the commander – a mistake had been made. I learnt the meaning of a gun. He stumbled, he didn't move; figures came towards us, loudly calling his name; they wandered aimlessly – they didn't expect to find him in the mist; they were a long way away – he was beyond reach. Not hearing anything, I thought of wild plans, the gun I had hidden; I wasn't sure – I got up and brushed my clothes, tired, uncertain. In the shouting and panic I dragged the body through a doorway, carried the load up two flights of steps. Every door was locked.

I was overtaken by medical officers. "You should not have touched the body." "I could not find anyone to help. I've been wounded." My arm was soaked with blood. The officer insisted that I cease work, led me away, ordered me to hospital. "This man has worked well." He demanded my name, which I had to give; he promised me a decoration; I was to be taken to hospital for treatment for shock. I had been an idiot – I had not followed the agreed plan; now I was being taken to hospital.

The doctor treated my arm. I had done useful work. I was put to bed. I slept for an hour. I woke, stared at the man standing over me: it was the sergeant of police. I had to think of some excuse. He wanted to know why I had not done as he had ordered. I told him I had lost my way; the lorry had left without me. There would have to be a fuller explanation – he was obviously suspicious. Maybe he was waiting for my brain to clear. He waited too long. The doctor returned; I showed him my letter of recommendation; he allowed me to go. There may have been suspicion, but the disaster had been an accident. At that moment a telegram was handed to me, inviting me to attend the funeral of a man cruelly assassinated by a fanatic. I was still wearing the uniform of the tall handsome man. The trousers were stained with blood – I had to wear my own trousers; they squeezed me into the coat, which gaped wide open in front; the hat would not stay on – I had to carry it under my arm.

In the morning the lines formed in the streets leading to the ground; the approach to the lines of cars led past houses;

we were watched from the gardens – the people watched in long lines behind the gates of their houses. He had been a young man, greatly liked. Protected by the neutral flag flying before it, my car drove with the others, surrounded by mourning crowds, to the desolate gardens. The commander was attended by men in magnificent uniform – they wore gorgeous dark blue and gold. I was introduced to the presence; he shook hands and talked with me. Encircled by death, walking the path between the stones, a long walk in a lovely forest, the daughter passed, walking slowly; at the sound of my voice she tipped the funeral flowers she carried to one side, using the leaves to screen her face, so that I saw the thick plaits but not her face. I went on as if I did not know she had passed. Opposite the wall the tall pine stood; the shooting had dealt a blow – he had fallen victim: the bullet had been wasted; the bullet had waited from the hour of his birth; he had been unable to protect himself.

A crowd had gathered to read the funeral notice posted in the entrance hall. I felt her hand. "Lean against me – it's cool." "I want to tell you…" She spoke in slow, carefully articulated words: "A mistake. The wrong man. You find it strange?" She said her father's men had fired the shots at random – part of their war of nerves – they were not concerned with whom they killed, as long as they killed. Her father had his own methods: the assassination was meaningful – the work of his brain – an excuse to wage sensational war. But she was trusted by the commander, and she would deal with him in her own way. "Get him in bed and stick scissors in his back. That's the method. We shall make sure of him this time." She took me to his room – she knew her way about – she showed me where they slept; she behaved like a wife; she said I could stay – I would not have to hide – I could sleep in their room.

# Chapter 8

HOLDING HIMSELF ABOVE HER, moving neither forwards nor backwards, the commander allowed her to survive; he turned with ease, mounted; just as he reached her, she shifted away – he pursued her; she shielded herself with her arms, facing him and crouching, she tried to escape; suddenly she turned towards him, hopeless – it was over. Failed, beaten, he continued in hope, really tired, not persevering; he did not share her panic – his exhaustion made it easy. As he woke, she prepared for a long fight; she was persistent; she stuck to her hate until it happened, but she was thrown off by his remaining motionless, by his motionless power. She endeavoured to close with him while she was strong – an amazing exhibition: she furiously hunted, grasped him; he flicked aside, he saved himself; she shifted to avoid the agony; it was driven home; there was no agony – he seized her neck and gave her a sharp hit at the base of the skull: it was over – swinging – no sound; she was overwhelmed; silence followed, clapping, whip-like, in the dense atmosphere.

With his height and weight he knelt on her spine; they fell with violence: her shocked face and flapping hands, her wrists against the wood; discoloured eyes, stains of earth and tears, bruised lips, cheeks splashed with tears; his dog between her feet, her feet in its belly; streaks of black across his face, his fingers. The short whip with a pellet of lead at the end of its lash; the hairs in his nostrils; the gaze of pleasure. The fourth stroke tore her skin – the patches of suffused blood were at first dark red; sharply defined injuries produced by blows, rupture, the skin dragged in a particular direction. She was aware only of some dazzling, some flattening; very slight, her red reflection; I could see the folded skin – the muscle dislocated, the normal state interfered with, altogether lost. Her body shook with frightened movements – the movements in her chamber, unusually deep – complicated, dragging. She fell downwards and inwards; it occurred several times – her body was dragged back; the nature of the pain was not understood, the pain in the stretched membrane remained; portions of the membrane stretched in fine threads, detached by a blow; the blood lay red and fresh, then black; a fly moved slowly across and came to rest; glittering spots, small particles of white, appeared in the blood and danced about with slightest tremor of the skin, lasted for several minutes and disappeared, leaving the surface wet.

No feet or stones – some soft thing, her head twisted sideways towards a basin of water. "Lie still." A fat face, poor child, a smell of onions; the marks of his teeth on her shoulders. She tried to stand up. He threw a handful of sweets towards her. "No." I saw her struggling; I touched her skirt. His fingers held her head, reached her elbows. I watched the pointed bones move, leant forwards and picked up her hand. I saw her teeth grinning – dim, squared shapes with a side still grey. I touched her mouth; he moved her arms and hands. I tried to help her – I saw her in the centre of the room, her throat, hair. "Her arm is broken," I said. "Very well – strap it to her side." He lifted her onto the bed; I watched the touching of the two of them, the specks on her fingernails, her white skin, freckled, reddened. They had both been hurt. He seemed taller, older. He set her arm in splints, bathed her mouth, brought a scarf for a sling. She bent down in front of him and, rather than look at her breasts, he turned his head away and examined the ironwork on the door. By their references to their childhood both seemed to have come from the same town. This irritated and depressed me. She ate from his hand; the feeding was done in silence – in his fingers the food became toys, coloured string, painted wood. He looked at her; they whispered; he kissed her face. No one spoke. He changed her bandages, trimmed the edges with her scissors. I handed her the scissors. She looked at me coldly: "You said?" "I? Nothing." He bathed the wound, touched her body, humming. He took the bandages from her arm. "There may be a scar." "Are you sure?" Her smooth face, pale mouth, thick hair. The ape was on her; I trained myself to watch.

When she was bitten by his dog, she welcomed it with a bowl of milk; she put in some sugar; the dog ate from her hand saturated with cream. She hung like a black thread round its neck, her hair round the roots of its ears; she spoke to it, confidently. Her sharpened scissors were three-quarters of an inch long, longer and sharper than they ought to have been, for needless pain was inflicted. She sat low so that she could stab freely; she stabbed hard, seized the dog's legs and twisted them so that they were dislocated, and it lost the lower joints as a result of this trick.

I did nothing at all. I avoided killing the minutest insect. I walked carefully – examined every seat before sitting on it. I wore muslin across my mouth. I counted fifty insects lying on the ground. I scrutinized every bit of dirt lest I should tread on and crush something.

I received word from her father of the plans being made outside. The advancing troops had surrounded an important town, and new attacks were planned.

She stood still in the centre of the room. We waited – I by the door, the commander asleep on the bed. She would not cut his throat with the scissors straight away, though nothing would have been easier. She said she preferred the continuous presence of death – the long sickness. She went to him like a dog a hundred yards away from a building; she sniffed the walls, then went away without eating. He placed ice in a bucket; she licked the frozen cubes. I reminded her of the plan we had made; I described the state of the war outside – the changing fortunes; I hinted at the prospect of revenge. She showed no response; concealed the scissors, while he watched, listened, watched the other, ready to dodge violent attack.

I went outside and started walking. I did not choose a direction, I could think only of what had happened to her, unable to believe that she had changed. I avoided the prisoners – I knew no one. I walked out of the camp without any idea where to go.

# Chapter 9

HER FATHER'S MEN HAD TAKEN half the country – they had moved from the hills towards the
town, so it was easy to make contact with them. I
was stopped and threatened by their frontier police. I
waited until the son came to me in uniform to thank
me for what I had done for him during his illness. He
was especially grateful that I had not betrayed him
to his father; he distrusted me, but recognized my
good qualities nonetheless. He was still a sick man.
He told me his father had refused his request to serve
with a fighting unit – instead he had been required
to broadcast propaganda speeches to the other side. I
remarked that this was responsible work – a compliment to his abilities – it would give him scope to speak
and write. He said he was incapable of writing, he
had never written a single word – he "spouted" what
others composed.

The father received me in his spacious and magnificent
apartment: there I found him, sitting in one corner,
near a window. I had remembered a more impressive
figure – he was not good-looking as in his photographs.
He wore the blue coat and darker blue trousers, his
well-worn clothes contrasted with those of his handsome son, an imposing figure in rich uniform, whose
hair grew low on his forehead, who wore armbands
and epaulettes, each with a knot of gold. I paid attention to what the older man said while he listened to

me closely; his penetrating mind at once absorbed the essence of each question; his answers were as sharp as a command. The son impatiently shuffled his type-written script as he prepared to rehearse before his father the speech he was to make later in the day. In accordance with custom, he began with compliments: "Within three months our leader will revolutionize the country, restoring it to its former high position among the nations. But if conditions are allowed to worsen, three years may be necessary for this task... Wounded in the trenches, oblivious to personal advan-tage, our leader has succeeded in creating a powerful party, but has remained a man of simple tastes. He is generous and warm-hearted. If he chooses to live austerely, it is to devote all his energies to his great work; he lives in a modest palace – the only diversion he permits himself is playing the violin; he does not drink wine, nor does he smoke; he never laughs; he entirely prohibits any projection of his own personal-ity; he is not only a clever, but also a good-hearted man; here is a man who resolutely puts the futilities out of his life, to leave place for nothing but work. A perfect gentleman – his charming wife, a clever son and pretty daughter complete the family group. His photograph, sent to all who apply, will be valued the more in the knowledge of how rarely he allows him-self so personal a gesture. He is unfailingly kind to visitors – he receives them in the spacious and mag-nificent state apartment; there they find him, sitting in one corner, near a window, paying close attention to what is said; his penetrating mind at once absorbs, his answers sharp as a command..."

I saw the son each day – it was a privilege to be his friend. He never failed to run after me in the street, calling a greeting until he attracted my attention. The father resented my close friendship with his son. He explained that there were those at that time who were in the highest positions, who had access to state secrets, and yet were known for their sympathies with certain persons. The son's high station made him difficult to deal with. An order was made that all letters were to be left open except those addressed to the leader himself. The repeated leakage of news to the commander made them suspicious and wary.

They accused me of failing to comply with certain regulations, though I performed my duties with straight-forwardness and strictest impartiality, whatever my sympathies. When they tried to prevent my reporting inter-views, if these were unfavourable, I pointed out that this prohibition constituted a breach of international law. They replied that they were not a party to these laws. Such lack of understanding I found disturbing.

Certain messages related to the manufacture of muni-tions. Finding that the son was anxious to earn large sums of money, I arranged transmission of these mes-sages through him. When he insisted that no message sent with his assistance should be against the interests of the country, I said that such requests confused the issue. He replied that, though he was and wished to remain a good friend of mine, he could not be a party to treason, and consequently it would be necessary to replace him. My conscience would not permit me to agree to this; my mission demanded his cooperation. I tried to persuade him that his work for me need not affect his other duties. I pointed out that he needed the money, which was his by right. I said to him: "I admire your character." I told him what he already knew – that this work was being done in other capitals by other envoys. I increased the sums allotted to him, and he was finally convinced by this argument. But there were further complications.

It was my custom to bring the morning papers to the father's office. I knocked on the door at the appointed time. The son was there. The storm was raging. "What do you want?" the old man demanded. "To give you these papers," I said, closing the door, never to open it again. I saw that nothing would change. For myself, I asked and received attention, I was promoted, but I realized that it was unwise to remain too long in foreign lands. The father was growing senile; one obtained favours only through his son, with whom one had to deal. Friends warned me that these were difficult and dangerous superiors to serve under, but for the time being I remained with them.

When a serious dispute arose between the father and the party, he let it be known that if his son was raised in rank, the matter would be settled in an acceptable manner. So it was done, although raising a young man to high rank was contrary to all custom. The father was old and unattractive, and his lack of success in war worsened his chronic bad temper.

It was impossible to rely on the son's loyalty. There were many who sold information. They knew no side but their own. I discovered that, while he was taking money from me for disclosing secrets, the son was at the same time gathering information on my movements. I was cautious;

my first duty was to preserve strict neutrality during those difficult days. When he asked me to work with him on a film he was to produce, I did not accept at once. I began to make enquiries. I found that both brother and sister were in the pay of both sides – that they exchanged secrets impartially. They had associates on the border, and messages were smuggled through several times before they were discovered.

The son should have paid with his life. He was jailed for fifty days, on suspicion. Then it was proved that he had been falsely accused by a real spy – a deserter taking his revenge when the son said he would not take part in his treasonable schemes, and had flatly refused to provide certain information. The son was released to continue his criminal, dangerous work.

The son came to me with a woman he called his nurse. He had been ordered to pay certain restaurant bills, but had left without paying. He had given my name and had been told that the man was unknown. I was annoyed by this feeble swindle. He then said he needed money to send to his sister. I promised to help. He returned within minutes to say that his sister had not received the money. I said it was impossible in so short a time. He said the money had been mislaid and produced a record of the correct sum sent. I said I would straighten the matter out by finding the money and repaying him. He would not accept this. I reasoned with him. He began to shout. I was obliged to call the police. He was furious. I could not understand him. He was one of the few I had trouble in dealing with.

He was accused of supplying troops with cocaine, and he was detained on this charge. He requested help through friends. But justice could not be interfered with. At that time no one cared or dared to tamper with the law. However, the accusations were proved false, by other events which later transpired. After he was caught and jailed, he dared to telephone me begging me to pay his bills, which of course I could not do.

The police planned his execution with unusual strategy. A senior detective was entrusted with the case. A friendship sprang up between them. They decided to escape to the frontier; police followed; they arrived; he grasped him by the throat: "You are detained as a spy. I am an agent of the political police." He was brought home and judged, expelled from the party and shot, protesting that he was a friend of mine.

His father announced that "the heroic defender had been taken prisoner after the demolition of the fort, after he himself had twice been wounded". I was there when the father learnt of the son's execution. He began to shout. "And they call it war!" It was a bad sign. I tried to interest him in the plans he had formed, the tactics he had originated. "What do we want maps for?" He snatched the maps from me. "We'll want maps. You'll see!" He unfolded the maps, replaced them on the table so that the battlegrounds lay face down; uppermost were the gentle hills and the sea, a fresh, unused blue. "I need a rest from this war. It's peaceful there." His finger pointed to a seaside town famous for its boredom and its waste. I said he should go there – the war would continue without him. His mood changed – to loud laughter and wild behaviour – I could see his son in him. A young soldier came in, from the son's detachment. He stood waiting. "Have you news?" "There's nothing left. No one." "What do you mean?" "The situation has not improved." He turned in military fashion, saluted and left. The father mumbled to himself. "These are details, details. He saw nothing, but that is not to say there was nothing. The man showed his blindness, that is all." I pointed out that the "skirmish" took place close to the frontier; his son could have escaped, though nothing would be heard for months; he could be posted missing – this was the normal procedure; he could be alive in another country. I was relieved when he interrupted me rudely: "That's nothing. I know that. You tell me nothing I do not already know." He continued talking to himself. "I used to shave every morning; now see what I will do. I used to eat meat, and fish. I cannot be the lover of another man – even my son." He staggered round the room; I insisted on helping him into his chair. I pushed towards him the model of the new piece of artillery with which his men were to be equipped, but he was not interested. He showed me again the photograph of his son in uniform. "Take a look at this. So you see. Better for him to have been shot than to be kept for ever in prison without trial. What could I have done to prevent it?" He stood beside the table; memorials of battles, tattered flags hung over the table. I spoke about his son's desire to go to the front. He answered: "He's disappeared. Finished." He went on to discuss tactics. "The strength of their artillery – and for defence we use sheets of tin! Tin is useless in modern warfare! We must improve our supplies of steel, or we'll all be blown to pieces! The leader must be cheered when he meets his troops; they attack with bayonets and are killed; the artillery goes on firing; they fight and are killed, hand to hand. The battle comes to an end. They cannot understand why it has taken so long, but if I have learnt the name of a village, it has been a necessary battle. I dream of the battle of annihilation. Kill them all, so there shall be none. Annihilation does not mean physical annihilation – annihilation means surrender, demoralization. A battle which goes on is not annihilation; annihilation means surrender. But these fellows fight. We must have artillery, the concentration of forces on one front, the direct blow against the enemy's decisive forces, tactics face to face with tactics – tactics orientated towards the offensive, tactics adapted to defence, to terrain and climate, based on the simultaneous use of weapons for defence and attack, in the pursuit of the enemy. Activity which knows no seasons gives an absolute tactical advantage over the enemy; the enemy is to be misled about our positions and dispositions, our defence in depth, our tank defence zones. Night will cease to be a time for rest – we shall break through at night over frozen lakes and rivers, we shall overcome by force as the result of superior tactics systematically applied."

My courage was upheld. I organized an office "to help the victims of war". A few friends assembled in my room. Hundreds of persons worked together; the organization was perfect – daily it dealt with missing soldiers, money matters, food – every detail of everyday life. We were in touch with both sides. We forced the belligerents to respect our neutrality. We gave of our resources, with punctilious impartiality, most lavish generosity. Wounded soldiers were met by ladies with drinks and cigarettes when their train stopped. So long as they travelled behind the lines, they were attended by ladies who served as nurses.

At a luncheon for sixty or seventy people to support the hospital for severe surgical cases, for the sick who could not be cured, I was the guest of honour. I could not speak. I attempted, without the aid of grammar. "What is he saying?" "You should be able to understand. I am endeavouring to speak your language."

A fine-looking man – the son, transformed, doomed to meet his death – stopped to talk to me on his way back. He had been dying on the battlefields. I invited him to lunch. I was filled with admiration for what he had seen. He ruined my velvet-covered furniture by scraping his greased boots over it. The incident gave rise to satirical verses. He was a troublemaker who tried to kidnap and kill, but the plan was found out; troops were summoned, with instructions to shoot on sight. So order was restored. A strike was called; no papers were printed; the town was still. I could not find out; men and women were falling; soldiers caught the disease; the schools were turned into hospitals; thousands died. Bread was sold by card. A relative sent me all I needed from home, but I could not cook the food – the people's police were free to enter. The drenching rain followed us everywhere. I found a room unoccupied, and there I sat on a chair. It was raining on the bright uniforms. Shivering, weary, unable to walk, ill and tired, I discussed plans for my return, and for the return of those who planned the commander's fall. They were willing to help me return, to simplify their own problem; they took care to protect their own. I was ordered to keep watch on the daughter – they suspected her. I waited for the long train carrying soldiers from one part of the country to another – men without boots, with no food; crowds waited for the train – they had to make sure of their places. I slept on the platform with a block of wood for a pillow. I could not sleep. The others slept and could not wake, and when they woke they shouted or wept. Because they could hate, apathy in death was easy. Indifferent, they celebrated hysterically, which intensified their indifference. They had worked but not owned, they had had no chance and no choice, no ration of life, no notion of danger, the threat to life, to their own. A mobile kitchen arrived, with soup and potatoes. After the crowd had had their food, they sang. I travelled with blinds drawn against all contact en route.

# Chapter 10

I ARRIVED BACK WITHOUT DISASTER. An hour later and I would have been caught in a storm. As it was, I was her guest. She was well clothed and well fed. She said she had been attacked: "He came in the night; the commander tried to set fire to my room." She was talking in an even more excited manner than usual. "He came last night and dragged me from my bed. I had to make room for some other women." Then came a long, involved story. At first she said three women were brought into the room, then it was five, then ten. I doubted whether any figure was the true one – it was not possible, it was not reasonable, to suppose it had happened.

She knew she was watched – she felt the breath on her neck – but she was ignorant of what was going on; she did not know she had been cruelly treated. I told her nothing – I left her alone on the other side of the room. She asked for my opinion; I gravely replied, going through the farce. She had suffered: she told me quietly about being in prison with dangerous neighbours mysteriously dying; the walled darkness; the sound of sighing; intricate and jealous people inserting poison under her skin. I smiled at her grotesque accumulation of horrors. She said: "It's true." She knew her father no longer trusted her, but she felt she had done all she had been asked to do. She would not believe her brother had died. She belonged to nobody, but she was under the control of two masters, imbeciles and idiots. I made attempts to help her – I brought her parcels of sweets and chocolates, cakes and all kinds of confectionery. Suddenly the gifts were stopped.

A picnic had been arranged. The weather was very cold. I received from the commander a box and a letter, a glittering gift. He was old and ill, hobbling on one leg – there was a wound in his foot which would not heal. "You must stay," he said. "We'll have a party." I noted his defeat, his age. No one enjoyed the party; we stayed indoors and played cards. He no longer had any hope, but he heroically went through the ordeal; although hatred had marked his face, his eyes showed no sign. He did not shake hands – he thought only about war; he did not want anyone; he did not want us to leave; he was helpless; he himself had to go; he wanted to shake hands with everyone, to remain part of things. He talked endlessly of his dogs: "I had the last one shot. He killed a prisoner, he pulled down an old woman – I had to have him shot. I am training his successor – I hope to get better results, but he is putting on weight." There was a note of insanity in his uniform, rich garments blazing with jewels, and the girl, who accompanied him, was gorgeously dressed. "The girl is my mascot; if I cannot bring her where I please, I will leave." There was a gasp. She was slow-moving and short-sighted; she found it difficult to see in the crowd; she followed him with grim persistence. The commander led us outside – we danced in the garden; from the camp hundreds of voices lifted; he urged us to enjoy ourselves. "You can go hunting. The organization is superb. The guests can choose. The shooting is done from the tower." "Kill for fun?" one of the guests asked. The commander did not reply; he blinked. I had an impression of yellow fire – the explosions of battle – as his troops retreated towards the camp.

He brought us indoors; we talked for hours in the great hall – the yellow-tiled roof supported by pillars, the darkened room lit by candles, the wax dripped over the gold. Each of us was presented with a medal with a piece of silk or skin attached to it, supposedly a ribbon. We were entertained by women playing music, keeping time with their bare toes. As there were no men, one woman played the part of a man. They looked like mushrooms, each mushroom a girl crouched under a hat, bending so they touched the ground. It was amusing to watch their backs; one lost her footing and rolled over – she was seized by the legs and pulled along. Divided from the women by the width of the room, the guards watched in silence. Two girls carried fire from behind a screen in iron dishes as tall as themselves; suffering magnified their limbs; no greetings, no word, the wind rising, their voices lamented; I could not distinguish one from the other; we went on eating, their breasts hanging over us like long potatoes. The sound of drums on stage confused with exploding shells outside; the building was roofed with tiles, the pillars painted, the walls streaked with lime. She was seated in shadow, her face oval in the dim room; she carried an umbrella, which she twirled to prevent any man staring at her; she offered me a bowl of milk, placing it on the ground at my feet; it was not necessary to know what she meant by the movement – there was no mystery – she used a poem to kill. The troops were outside – there was no time for marriage; I gave her some clothes, but she would not put them on – she sent them out of the room. Because she had been bitten by one of the dogs she kept her face half hidden. I had only to wait; the idea was to do nothing at all. The stage was a fortress surrounded by a wall, loopholed; on either side were piles of grenades for the last troops who kept guard. The crumbling of the place brought out the rats and other vermin; circus dogs dressed in yellow, wearing caps, trotted on money. Her hunger was so strong, her flesh was like earth that disappears; with her skirt held up she ran with the spotlight, she scrambled for paper and rubber; there was no space; she had no form; she drifted in the strong light; in the haze of dust her face was white, her body bare; she wore no jewels; I had no desire at all. She was ashamed of the ugliness of her legs – a feather had been tied to each ankle; her head swung from left to right – she pretended to be absorbed – staggered round. The commander said: "Duties are taught to the girls. They used to live by making mats, now they are kept alive and not ill-treated." Her answer was a smile – indifferent, divine as an almond. An explosion shattered the lights, brought tiles and plaster crashing onto the stage; the commander brought torches and placed them near her; her legs with gestures invited me to enter. I put on my coat. She sang a song, waved a flag, advanced, stumbled against the dark walls; I could see her feet in the rubble and dust – the two legs blazed white, the heavy head hung on the long neck, inconceivably slender.

In silver, infinitely high, the commander raced by in one of his great cars. White cloths were spread on the ground; women shouted – they were forced into doorways – women made themselves into wheels. She ran with them, stones swinging above her lips; she threw flowers through the windows. The commander stopped for her, rode with her, a rug around his shoulders as big as a town and tipped with metal. They walked across the wide plain, a wind blowing vast blue – his gigantic forehead, her eyes splashed with gold, dogs in a gale, lost in its sugared darkness. Her hair was unclipped, touched with dyes, decorated with blue beads; she wore a collar loosely round her neck; on her back embroidered stripes of yellow and blue; a cap on her head; her long hair parted in the middle, scented and sleek.

He allowed her to search the mouths of the dead – the gold in their mouths was increasing in value. She brought her dead to the river, where they were torn by fishes; perhaps I had never seen them seven feet away – I saw each move; I watched; during all that eventful time I saw nothing impossible. He had to train her in the work. She came to deliver his share – he tried to take one from her; she refused to part with it; there was noise, face to face, each grasping the dead, with feet fixed, to get more. He took it; she got away with the gold from the teeth – she hid the bits of gold in her own mouth; this annoyed him – he grabbed at her mouth, got a hold on the tongue; she shrieked, dragging – at last she freed herself – she dragged herself away. He went on as if nothing had happened. She was left wandering, unable to feed herself, away from the others, her mouth a mass of cotton wool; oblivious to what was happening, they sat close together again and watched the flies round the bodies. The food cry was heard and the heads went up; the cry repeated time after time. Disturbed, she gave the cry, went up to the body and touched it, dragged it down as the others crowded round, clamoured for it, each one desperate for it. She wrenched off the leg, jabbed it – thick end first – into her mouth, tried hard to swallow it, could not get it down; the thicker part became less visible – there was nothing but the foot; she twisted off the protruding foot. Holding the body, she twisted it, with a cutting and pulling action; with a final twist the limb was removed. She knew how to do it. The limbs were small; then they increased in size, and became too large – then only the rats dared to go; the rest were left starving. The commander's voice was heard; she crept into a sheltered corner, close to him.

The cages were broken – the crowd had got loose and invaded the shops. Though they picked up weapons, they remained victims – blind, breaking down, drowning. They were driven out between the roofs; the crowd cried slaughter – they had a passion for picking things to pieces; they found crowbars; they moved with plunder; grew to great size; fought for a place of power; they had no leader – were angry, with a new kind of headlong terror – a clumsy plunging and bounding. The old man's face was red, overfed. One hand hung, his face terrible. They watched his face in order to defeat his plan. He had failed to find others to carry him. He threw them bread, but they did not run for scraps. He went into the street and stood whining, spent time sitting and looking at the rain. They rushed at him from opposite points, two or three at a time. He was not allowed to reach home. He dashed back between walls; in sweeps and curves and rushing and collision he shook them off. He used his nails, a stone. They circled round, five yards from the walls. His favourite dog had gone – I had seen him tormenting the dog who hated him; the dog had learnt to watch. He peered in at windows, at the heat, longing for the fire. Someone threw a stone, and in a minute a dozen others followed. They chased him with shouting – they tried to kill him by grinding his head on a stone, rubbed it on the ground, split the skin of his forehead and crushed one of his ears. Without her help he could not reach home. She sprang on him, opened his mouth, scooped out the spit while he chattered. He had to wait till she had finished or went mad. She put on prisoners' clothes, mounted the goat; they came closer; he glanced at her with begging eyes. She threw him backwards, leaping; he struck the hot embers piled together, dropped, received in the face the hot coal. She started laughing; he filled his fist full of clear glass, passed a slow hand down, lost interest, waited. He would kill himself. She slit his nostrils. The final sound when they slit. And when they slit it was impossible. He received blows from thick sticks – he staggered round, blind with blood; exhausted, he fell against a cage, dragged himself through the electric wires; for a moment he was confined in a dome with an iron floor – it was painful to touch the electrified metal; he crashed through the glass and was seized on the other side. They put sticks into his mouth – little by little he died, disfigured. He was tied to a post; sticks were thrown at him; they would kill him in the end; he was not left to bleed to death – he was maimed, spreadeagled on his back; forked pegs held down his hands and feet; he cried slaughter; others attacked him and held him down; he cried slaughter – their cry; he was beaten to death in the dark, given the name of stone, shaved and blackened, hung by his feet from the branch of a tree.

This punishment was inflicted – that is how he was treated when he was too old to be of any use. His foot may have been cut off with a heavy knife and put into his mouth. Presumably it would cause his death. If not, the throat was cut.

A horse galloped in the street; the hall collapsed; the walls were not intact – the old walls had fallen – there was nothing left. There were the feet of two stone monuments, the left inscribed, the right without writing; the central block had a square of iron remaining – the rest had disintegrated; there would be no restoration. The old man and the old woman were no longer in existence – those old people found on the corners of streets; they were too frail – they were wiped out when disaster came.

I concealed myself close by, cut off from the crowd. Nothing happened. He remained motionless – his brains had probably, without warning, dropped to the ground. He remained; stillness maintained; there was no cause to walk across the intervening inches; stillness maintained for hours, except for slight alterations of the eyes. The eyes were closed at times. I saw his head – long, rounded, the trunk projecting beyond the grey head, finely lined; bristles around the mouth; the outer bristles tipped with white; the effect extraordinarily twisted – serrated like the teeth of an iron comb – the comb used to clean the bristles around the mouth. We stayed close for hours – two enemies; my eyes passed over the bits of twisted wood, the edges of which – little bits of brown and grey bark – represented discovery through half-closed eyes. He was not far away – wounded, crouched, sinking; he could have stood up. I saw him laid on the stones like a bit of stick, bare earth underneath, some kind of resting place – leaf mould, bracken crushed flat by the weight. His skin was dull grey turning white, barred and streaked, pencilled with grey. Our two bodies placed side by side were small, hardly to be seen – bits of stone or grit which the eye passed over.

# Chapter 11

P EOPLE PUT ON THEIR best clothes and went into the
streets; they put on fancy dress, they wore headdresses
and capes, and came and went, offering congratulations
to one another. People like roaming dragons, people in
furs like flowing water: their noisy shouts filled the streets,
they opened shops and began business. Their lights were
lit, scattering lantern flowers, scattering customers – a
hundred thousand lamps were lit at night, scattered on
stoves, the gates, the doors, convenient blocks of stone.
Like fireflies, stars, to the sound of drums they were put
out under silk coverings with floating banners and small
objects carried in front: artificial flowers specially made,
flowers of all seasons, with painted scenes moulded out
of ice and from cheap tin imported from abroad, and
from shoots of wheat by order, symbolic figures of men
and animals. All shops displayed her father's face – each
window larger than twelve by twelve held a photo of his
face – her father's face in every street in frames of wood,
in frames of silk and glass, with small pieces of silver and
gold secretly put inside. The night was filled officially, with
official fireworks of every variety imported from the east,
three hundred small boxes, a thousand flower pots, fifteen
fire-and-smoke pools, twenty-two thousand rockets, ten
peonies strung on a thread, forty plates sprinkled with
water, twenty golden plates, thirty pinwheels, thirty falling
moons, dozens of flags of fire, fifteen hundred double-
kicking feet, a thousand fire crackers which exploded on

the ground and then again in the air, ten explosions flying to heaven, five devils noisily splitting apart, ten bombs for attacking the city, eight eight-cornered rockets, a hundred lanterns of heaven and earth, twelve silver flowers, twelve trees of fire – the sounds dinned the ears, the flashes darkened the eyes, the dust from the feet gradually lessened, the shadows fell stretched on the ground.

She cut out coloured materials and put them on her head; she ran through hoops to the sound of a gong; she made small cakes for her father. He made her stop her needlework for fear that it might injure her eyes – she made umbrellas out of coloured paper. She sat talking to me, her hand on an animal – she had a dog of her own; when she had pains in her ears she touched the dog's ears; when she could not see, she touched his eyes; when she had broken bones in her feet, she stroked his feet. She cut out of stone a channel for running water in the form of the face of a dog, and she floated cups down the stream to other children waiting below.

Her father took charge. He ordered the commander's death to be marked by two stone monuments, a stone platform, a stone column eight feet high surmounted by four banners inscribed in four languages, iron-coloured tiles, an iron covering. A bell was cast. It was fifteen feet high and fourteen in diameter; the knob of the bell by which it was suspended was seven feet high; the thickness of the iron was seven inches. It weighed twelve tons. It was carved with characters inside and outside: the characters were each an inch in size, and close together like the teeth of a comb; they were written by a scholar; they echoed the words written on the banners. One banner asked: "What is religion?" Three banners answered: "Fear." The bell was suspended. The tower was levelled and the bell buried in the ground. The bell was removed. A second tower was constructed, fifty feet in height: it was square below and round above; there were windows on all sides; a circular staircase ascended on the left and descended on the right; each stair was carved; above the bell sprawled a bronze dog being knifed by a man; the bell hung in the centre – pure bronze, exactly upright, with a fine sheen. I never heard it sound. It was the year of hope not to be realized – not for years, not in the way expected.

Her father ordered the completion of the bridge – the bridge that had been begun before, the bridge that had been talked about, the link between the old town and the new. It was nothing unusual. The bridge crossed the river, it passed the town; there was nothing, then it ran – it was impossible to prevent. There were tunnels, a strip of metal; it carried; it was built; rocks were moved and heaped up under mountains; the bridge was built in terror, the work was finished with songs – she sang; the earth was moved, step by step – filling bags with earth, she worked. Other hands attempted – failed; she stayed there, bending. She longed for a jug of milk; a drink of water was the taste of apple in her mouth, a touch on the shoulder, a smile. She picked up a piece of sacking to wipe her hands; it was soaked in oil – it made her hands glisten. She worked for thirty hours, alternately lashed and praised. Her brain was nailed in a box.

Her father shouted, his voice against the noise, boastful of the labour and colossal expense, the cubic yards and thousand tons. She struggled, a patch of sweat under her lip.

She slept close to his animals, his valuable hounds. In the corner of her room she kept a dog, kissed his teeth – she adored his sharp teeth; clinging to his teeth she turned, falling onto a sloping table. I said: "Something of yourself." "And so?" she replied. "Was it not you?" Her face began to speak of home. She had returned to her family, waving her hand; then a piece of lead replaced her slow hand; her lips moving, she came towards me. We did not meet – she had no reason to tell the truth. She left, motioning with her hand towards my cool recess, a table placed between columns, pieces of furniture within an archway, musical instruments, elegant clothing, gentlemen gazing at lakes.

She worked on the line. She took the risk, by regulation forbidden, when the smoke came, to leap off the line. She came to me. A sinister fact. It was the rule to choose to do without. She jumped and clung to her need for the new. There was no wall, no wire, but terror was their weapon; there were all the signs; the blocks were kept ready in huts. The rest were imprisoned by the familiar, the family wall.

I was not bound by their regulations. I asked for information. I was told that the work could be seen in steel. I measured the steel and asked again. I was referred to the inspectors; I saw none.

She lifted the wheel, walked in a circle, prevented the wheel from slipping back. She worked on the hardest roads, her skin a blanket, a leather bag; she could not drink water; her comfort lessened; she scraped the hillside; she was thrown, slipped down; her feet caught; she lay like a stick on the ground. Drivers passed in rock-filled trucks; lines of trucks on the roads, the rock path; rock blast, engineering to the end that two towns should be joined by a bridge, a railway track, a great high road. Watchmen guarded the iron; they did not notice her while the trains were in motion with a wild air – brass encased in patterns of brick red and black with pieces of mirror, crowned with iron and patterns of red, with a high front, brass lower down, tints of bright lights and wide areas of iron clapping against metal or wall, rock, iron held in fire, wheels working, streaks daubed on cement walls and the name branded on stone – her family name – slate-tinted, slab-sided, gaunt and hideous beacons of usefulness hurling themselves over walls.

I heard her breathing. She refused my help. I could not protest or protect as she scuffled past, hollow, narrow, unknown. She had shaved her head; she was dry earth, burnt grass, blackened wire, torn and scrubbed; she worked on uneven ground, crawled, moved, marched, portrayed the work – a show of work. She led the shouting; all messages and questions sounded sinister, and shouting was greeted with cheers and shouting. She carried her shoes round her neck – she would not wear shoes; her yellow shirt was red with sweat because of rage; her sweat stinging, her skin dotted with a fine white growth, she alternately drooped and shouted. On a platform a propaganda man – plump, with white teeth – his full mouth quivered with laughter; beneath the poster the torn remains of an early proclamation... inviolability of person and dwelling, unlimited freedom of religion, speech, press, assembly, strikes and unions, freedom of movement and occupation, election by the people of army officers and recall of any of them, at any time, by the will of the majority of the electors, replacement of the police and the standing army by a general arming of the people, eight-hour workday for all hired labour – allowing, in case the work is continuous, for not less than one hour's time for eating, complete prohibition of overtime work... She threw away her shoes, unwilling to be the one with shoes; she was sweating, her body closely covered with grey cloth. The bones of her face were still good. I had eyes. "When I leave, will you come with me?" I was about to say more, but that was sufficient. Slowly she began to lose control. "I've had enough." Her eyes inflamed. There seemed to be no danger; calm was a sign of strength. "I could not do so – I might want to – the frontier's closed." I pulled her down in the heat; there was no room; the roof moved, the ground was forced up, her knees touched the ground – the skin was hurt by the stones; she was forced to stay in that low place – she tried to get away, but was jerked under.

Friendship was survival in the face, the rock foundations of the bridge and the songs moved forwards slowly. She organized the dance; they followed her, shouting in time, circled the fire, died down, sat and slept by the fire. Some were accused of sabotaging labour discipline. They were expelled by soldiers with bayonets drawn, piled into lorries and driven off at top speed. We built brick structures; the earth was loaded, the rock tipped; the earth rose up, compressed by stamping. The towers of bricks held the weight of the bridge, which would open by swinging or lifting – a counterpoise bridge supported by beams resting on abutments on either side, having lattice girders, a hanging scaffold, a railed plank extending. She wheeled a load of stones along a path of planks; her feet were bandaged – the bandages on her crippled feet were tied with cords. I observed her straining her legs forwards, stumbling over the wheelbarrow, her movements as she practised moving forwards in bounds, her convulsive grip and struggling climb, the proud look on her father's face; he appeared at ease on the observation platform, but wanting nerve. For the first time he climbed down; his clean shoes sank in the clay; he held her arm firmly; he was in a good temper; she had to climb the slope at speed – he helped her up. He was sixty-eight years old, short and stout, with a round flushed face, with a pipe the feature of his dress in all his portraits, the hand covered the pipe. The detective who always stood behind turned hastily, entangled his sleeve in the sleeve of the leader; the pipe fell to the ground; those surrounding him formed a close circle, and the damage was repaired. She was not trying; she kicked at the loose stones, she struggled up the floor of rock – a long slope with sides of stone, stones pulled off a wall, a new wall built over the mountains, a line across a map.

I walked carefully along the track, made a map of the new line where it paralleled the frontier for twenty miles and branched south-west a few miles from the town. The workers were sent in trucks from the town to the camp; they crossed the track at two points. Heavy supplies in armoured trains travelled at dusk or at night. I hid at night and watched the guard through a window in order to note when he left his post. The door opened, he looked in my direction, walked back towards the bridge; the man failed – his back was turned when he was meant to guard.

The skilled dynamiters split the rock more slowly in the last hour of work. The great rock shook. A ruined engine with roaring coals crashed into the shattered trucks; twisted metals flung the trucks with violence on their sides, an ammunition truck loaded with shells exploded, in two places the track was obliterated by splintered rock. I saw her running in the middle of the track – she escaped a collapsing wall; two others were killed. One armoured train had been derailed, twenty-three trucks turned over by the explosion. My job was done. I should have cleared out at once and returned home, but I could not leave the dozens of men on the ground; foolishly I went to help the dead – I worked at speed, rounded up rescuers and cranes. I opened the gates, held them open, cut the ropes across the road; as they fought to get free of the wreckage, they threw themselves over the rubble. The wind raised clouds of dust from the rubble, then the dust was laid by rain. I was not wearing shoes; my bare feet slipped on the moistened dust on the rotten planks which led to the bridge. The bridge was cut in two – half lay in water, half on land. I leapt across a strip of water; I tried to reach her; it was dangerous; water was already flowing between my feet. I was sixty yards away – it was unsafe: water ran down the wall; the roof started to give way; I was forced against the wall; it was useless to try – I turned back; I was trapped by a rush of water; it was hard to keep my balance; I steadied myself and waded through; I pushed against water up to my mouth; I felt her with my hand – I leant against her; I could not keep awake. I saw furniture – the room was mine: the front room, the living room; words could be heard, someone was walking; there was only one; the wind blowing the dust. I went through rooms to go to the lavatory; I knocked the light over; I could not put my foot on the ground, I could not open the door; I lit the lamp – the glass was broken – it was not safe; the light went out; the glass fell to pieces. No light showed the way – lamps would not keep alight in water. Listening to the water rush, I felt for the plank, crossed the darkness. Stones fell from the roof; I heard the stretcher crack – it made no difference. I was careful to crouch. The others were hurrying back to warn us; they delayed us. Her desperate face: "I have no pay. I have not worked a full week. I have made a bad start."

# Chapter 12

S HE WAS AN ASSET to the state. If they discovered her attempt to escape, she would be taken back immediately, and I would be carrying dynamite if a shot should strike my back. There was a safe area a mile to the south of the town, well away from view at night; from there it would be easy. There was a moon. I was confident. The guard was lying dead – I would be him returning home, my papers in order. I carried the actual papers of a real man, including the photographs of his girl. Silently we crouched by the side of the road; the broken moon gave light; there was nothing; a whisper. I could explain everything to everybody. I was complete. We lay down by the hedge until it was light. The weather was very cold. They would not know where to look.

The straight white road, the trees by the side of the road, the man mending the wall, the narrow poles with white faces turned backwards and forwards from the town; we left the road to see the slabs of rock.

On a ridge of boulders – a hut of boulders frozen over – we set about building a shelter: we made a tent by drawing together the edges of a piece of cardboard, with a slanting roof as a precaution against falling stones; we worked together to weave a tent to shelter a whole family. Drawn together, essential to each other, we slept covered by tough sheeting to keep out the cold and preserve the warmth generated by our bodies.

I returned home with food. We sat and repaired our home. I was putting on my boots when men approached us and asked us what we were doing there. They could not understand our language. We had to wait while they checked our papers. I said we were there to admire the palaces and see the fortress pulled down.

She knew she was threatened with capture. She had been given her freedom after being kept locked in for years, and in the end liberty would lead again to capture. Some troops approached – a company of fifteen, part of a regimental band – whose music we had heard before, not far away. One of them played the clarinet; the wood shone black in the sunlight. She kept apart from them; I diverted their attention from her by conversing with them. I learnt that in the plains below for some days there had been heavy rains – the floods were out – with the result that some troops had been drowned, valuable equipment had been abandoned, one of their dogs could not be found, the families of some of the men had lost their homes. Their senses were dulled, their powers reduced; they stood on the ground trying to practise the same tune. Two young drummers sat on the stone wall a few yards away, demoralized, helpless. They tapped out the same rhythm over and over again. One of them undid the heavy leather harness and placed his drum beside him on the wall. He was warned by an officer: "You could be shot."

A yellow bar of light dissolved; we lay on the rough sand, the last light of the sun in her mouth. A footstep warned. We retired quietly into the depth of our home, to lie low. She would have run, flown. But her injured, tired body was incapable, due to her slight build, her habit of running, the painful shocks she had had. I told her it would be better, more effective, to hide. We enclosed an area on which she could lie flat on her back – an area protected on all sides by a series of stones raised to form a sort of diamond, irregular but strong, with a vein of stone running across obliquely to the outer edge. She lay back, safe, and smiled with her fine teeth. Her head lay in a small clear area where the sand was a dark colour and the stones made a straight edge, hard and sharp. With flint I entirely removed the roughness where the grains projected. We were not alone in bed. Built around us in successive layers were old patterns, fixed in design, immovable without breaking the body.

I used my hands to alter the ground, the patterns, until we reached perfection, giving complete smoothness around us both, to our eyes an indescribable beauty, magnificent, costly. The strength of each stroke was the slow and careful elaboration, the only style which had success. My hands used her like an object, carried her forwards. She judged my caresses by their weight – the lightest being the best. I felt a vibration between us – we communicated – and though we no longer completely overlapped, a space was formed, enclosed: the outer surface formed a box. I moved slightly in – tentative, intermittent, then more restrained. Suspicious, she appeared to recede. Then the two were exactly symmetrical; in our peculiar bends and convolutions we corresponded perfectly. I left her easily, attempted again without success; certain muscles hardened in that position, then attained the perfect state. With unusual patience, without injury to the delicate structure, we found the desired position. She seemed not quite happy, to be making a conscious effort, by crossing one leg over the other so that the position became unintelligible. Then everything – the sand, the rocks, the structure of the building enclosing us – everything was used, until that time, and another time, became equally perfect. If a part went dead and had to be moved, the suggestion was reversed, and the same seemed the same. She was quite silent. Her love came from joy. She invited me to come to her – expected me to come and join her. I was unable to discover any fault. I remained quiet – carefully, she saw me retreat, quietly – she remained quiet. I went towards her again, merely for my own pleasure, for the pure joy of life. It was interesting to attempt to force her to retreat into her own dwelling, and find both of us in one home.

Hearing songs, I thought they were being broadcast, but the band was being drilled – marching and countermarching into itself. We were near the end – the outside was closing in on us. She covered her legs. We could both appreciate the music; the band was making itself a life – we were swamped by the big sound of the band. She was seen: she wanted to sit in the sunshine to hear the music and watch them exercise their dogs. She had grown young: she was not lined in any way – her skin had been carefully smoothed. We had only just room to turn round; our building, commenced at the beginning of winter, was merely a winter shelter – not right for the spring; though I could have enlarged it, perfected the smoothness of its walls, it was still not a home – merely a shelter. The whole of the labour had been performed, but the place must now be left and the labour wasted. I knew that, though she did not. We were really in the earth, simply lying on the surface of the earth. She pushed off the roof, like a lid. It was not a question of escape, but of moving.

She listened to the cries of the dogs, stretched after us, moving in leaps. Fleeing from the dogs with the speed of a greyhound, her life a struggle against attack, she knew how to reserve her strength when running. She kept ahead just enough to avoid being caught. Occasionally dodging to one side or turning suddenly, she changed her direction and followed their steps, jumped a gate, forced through a hole in a fence, leapt five feet, running at full speed. She escaped by mingling with them.

We climbed a higher – far higher – rock, more dangerous; falls of a hundred feet led down to ledges of terrifying steepness. We stood on the edge of a chasm. A gun was fired at the foot, at the legs. With bewildering sounds of thunder and splashes of blood on the rocks, they left a dog dead on the ground. Like a ship covered with hair, the teeth quite small, the eyes large, the inner surface blank. It appeared blind, the power drawn from its eyes, facing a storm of rain. I used a handkerchief to clean its eyes. We made a grave in the shelter of a bush. She scratched away the earth.

She did not feel sorry for herself; she did not care. She dug a hole and knelt in it. She waited for hours – she did not know whether she was falling asleep or dying – then an inner change occurred; she began to murmur. She underwent a peculiar transformation, dashed about in fits of wildness in the middle of the afternoon. She made a sudden rush down the hillside; about a quarter of a mile away from me she turned towards the guns – they came out to meet her before she had a chance to turn. "Best to hide! Don't risk being killed!" she shouted to me as she ran.

Cleverly she crossed swampy ground and doubled back towards the town. She taught me the art of lying motionless on the ground to avoid being seen. She showed me how to feed on milk sucked from a feeding bottle; we stole a few garden vegetables and scraps of meat left lying on the ground.

We were challenged by a guard. I heard her inward grunt, pathetic scream. "The only way, the open fields." I held her arm. I showed my papers, told my story. The hour was marked on the papers; two or three of them, each with a different date. The guard was in a hurry – he had no time to investigate. I considered this man. He was not satisfied. I had made a mistake: I had hesitated to declare myself. I said we were returning to the town. We walked around, uncertain of our direction.

# Chapter 13

I T COULD HAVE BEEN ANY TOWN, on either side.
Squads of soldiers marched the streets in rapid time,
drilled, disciplined, yet at moments, where the road
divided, uncertain which way to march. The way back
to the bridge was barred by a lorry loaded with coiled
barbed wire. We went to the nearest café, moving in
the direction indicated by the police. We were trying
to reach her father's house by a roundabout route; we
were disturbed, and everyone knew it. I thought we had
found the house. I saw no sign – maybe we were too late.
Information about the escape would by now have reached
her father. I had been too talkative.

The front door of one house was slightly open. I had no
hesitation in entering. Her father was at home, eating. I
asked the old man whether we might stay for the night. I
said I wanted to return home, I wanted peace and quiet.
I whispered to him that I did not wish the police to know
– they might ask questions, although I had a proper
explanation. He said he wished to talk to his daughter
alone, but I remained. They, on the other side of the
room, sat and talked in his bedroom; she sat on the edge
of his bed. "I want to speak to you," he said. I could not
hear the reply, only the sound of his feet shuffling on the
floorboards. His low voice: "I knew he was not what he
appeared to be. You should have come to me." She asked
him: "What has happened? Why are you living here?" The
shuffling stopped. I looked at the door. Then a slurred

sound, not like speech, a different sound: his voice, but his voice changed – high-pitched, almost singing. "The building was in perfect condition; as my official residence it belonged to the people, not to me, yet heavy bills for furnishing and repairs were presented. I sent them back; they were returned for signature; I refused to sign. I knew nothing about repairs – there had been no repairs. Every pressure was brought on me; they begged me to talk to the press; I allowed myself to be persuaded, but after one tumultuous interview I knew I had made a mistake – the reporter had been carefully chosen as one who could be made to serve their purpose. I signed a joint statement for our mutual protection, setting out the facts of the matter, but after his article had been published, he disappeared. Then, one day, smiling his vacant smile, my deputy handed me a copy of the paper. I glanced at the paragraph, I understood I was to be accused of a crime against the state. Anger is no weapon against power. I consulted old friends, well-known men, but control lay in other hands. I learnt that my removal was the price for the setting aside of a menace to the party's power. So I was involved in the party feud; my career was of no importance – the matter was to be arranged between them. I was advised to tell my story, and I did so. But unrest was increasing, and personal problems faded before the emergency. I was promised that, as soon as I resigned, the wrong would be righted. I submitted. I went to them and was welcomed, but one of those men warned me. I knew his advice was wise; I had not yet heard the end. I came to rid myself of my power. My old friend was asked for an explanation; he attempted to defend himself, saying I had been ungrateful – he had loaned me sums of money and had not been repaid. I could not answer. I wrote a letter. Fear of the new man was so great. I was tried for treason. My opponents were powerful, connected by family with other politicians; they were feared by many; it was useless and dangerous to fight them. I would lose my case. I was avoided, followed by spies, a prisoner in my house. I still believed I could win. I had cheques proving it was I who had loaned the money. I was acquitted. I won my last victory there. I had been persecuted; a letter had been written to the judge by the Ministry of Justice – he was 'interested in the maintenance of judicial dignity'. My adversaries sought a sentence condemning me to exile – if only for one day; it would have been sufficient to break my power. On the day for the trial of the prosecutor's appeal the court was ready. I called my lawyer. He was not in court! A search was ordered. I could not understand his failure to appear at the last moment, before the court of last resort. I demanded that they acquit me – I was obliged to do so; I demanded payment of my costs. Each spoke in turn. The prosecutor said he would take my argument for his own; he would not speak of costs – I had borrowed from the people, and their debt demanded to be repaid. I became ill; I asked to be allowed to speak – I repeated my request. My lawyer had had in his possession a slip of paper containing conclusive evidence, the full explanation of all questionable transactions – the paper was delivered to him so that it could be examined. The usual procedure had been followed, but the clerk entrusted with the work had apparently overlooked an important item – he had abstracted the slip from the file and kept it. With this conclusive evidence in his hands he had sent word to the lawyer on the other side and had said that he would without hesitation publish this overwhelming proof of the injustice of the accusations and appear as witness for the defence. I had asked him to show me the precious document; he had done so, but had not allowed me to take a copy of it. I had set down our entire conversation on the back of a letter which my lawyer had kept among his papers. This trial has meant the loss of my home. I have been obliged to remain here under police surveillance – they made it easy for me to go elsewhere, but the dense bureaucracy prevented this, and, anyway, I knew it was better to remain. This was the result desired by my adversaries, and their tactics may keep me here for years; my agony is due to my own actions; I have tried, wanted; my years are clouded, but I have kept alive."

Voices outside: voices gave instructions concerning luggage for dispatch by train, the handing-over of letters for personal delivery. "Give... immediately you... ocean... funds." One foot across the step, I heard her shout; I twisted to look across. "Thank you for choosing me to be the one to come with you." I saw that same individual, criminally stupid. "Goodbye." Her fingers digging into my arm. "The wheels won't go round." The words in her throat, staring at a lunatic. Her face did not even know the essentials. She laughed. Her manner became quite different. I remembered that I was not supposed to know the meaning of the journey. A word, a look, a kiss, a scarf, a sleeve, those white arms, thick red hair, her father, his crushed face; he grinned as he watched – he had trapped wolves and buried them. I saw his face twitch. "She has disappeared." "You mean she flew." Alone in his room her hands seemed helpless, fingering ribbons, her wet eyes singing of murder, her body among red and green embroidered cushions, a wasp sting on her cheek, a pity, sad. Bending forwards, I kissed her hair; her voice was cut off; she fell; I held her.

Sixteen miles from the town I lifted her onto the train. We travelled together towards the frontier. She became violent. "Never again abuse those who welcome you, or judge when you have shown yourself ignorant. When you get home, find that out for yourself." Anger in her eyes. "We shall continue the life we are used to. We feel free. Look at the map, and try to understand why." An underlying layer of jealousy. "I don't see." I pushed the girl towards the train, climbed onto the leather seat; we flew towards the gates, the cracked light, brass, blood. We drove, continuously changing, with hollow trees, drowned in rivers, one hand to shade her head, with the other testing the balance of a whip.

There were no cars waiting outside the station. "It is too cold. You can't expect them to wait." Another train, this time unheated. There was no light in the coach nor in the whole length of the train, though the windows were intact. We sat on wooden seats in the dark, in the cold. She showed a knowledge of politics far in excess of mine. We discussed her father's programme – a subject about which I had the haziest ideas. Three hours later they managed to get the steam working. We slept: a triumph.

Fresh coffee and bread were provided at the frontier town. There were two stalls for coffee, so that when one was handing out hot drinks, the other was boiling a fresh supply. Once more we heard the commander's name – the name that was disturbing the country. His friends had gathered others who shared his views.

Hours to wait for the night train, we explored the lovely town – streets shaded, iron walls, the superstructure of a sunken ship caught lengthways across the mouth of the harbour, the coal-dark sea, silent, alert, the coming night, change of light, the night filled with basketwork chairs. Our argument about wealth. Her small fist on the book, splitting the pages. "For the last five years we have been very orderly and well disciplined. We have become organized. The only bridge across the river is a temporary construction. Everyone wonders whether it will stand the rush of ice in the spring. Work on the other – partly demolished – bridge is planned, to be completed in July." In comparison with the harbour, the town had not suffered much: houses were still windowless, bookshelves bare, laboratories devoid of apparatus, but this was to be expected. She stepped onto the street, sucking an ice cream. "I assume you are interested, though I know you are from a wealthy land." She persisted in continuing the conversation. I said: "I'm starting home tonight. If you agree, I should like to photograph the spot where the commander was killed." The scene of the crime was pointed out with her customary charm, politeness and generosity. This sort of reaction made it difficult to hit out. He was dead, a sore on his mouth, no mark on the pavement in the peaceful street. Meanwhile, several iron-hooped packing cases on which there were many curious marks and growths attracted her attention. She examined a length of brown paper which she pulled out through a gap in the sewing by slitting the tightly stretched canvas with the sharpened blade of a pair of scissors. A rolled rectangular piece of brown paper; she told me she could tell its origin: "The place from which you come".

We ate a cheerful supper in a brightly lit restaurant. Bells rang and were answered by bells. We strolled about, her hand on my sleeve. She stared at a shabby monument – the statue of a soldier, a brother, a kneeling man. There was an inscription; it was impossible to read. We wasted the day, though we had been warned not to. The trams were running; people walked to work in lit streets – they looked at their wristwatches by the light from shop windows. She liked whatever I gave her – a length of steel, a leather case. She stood in the doorway and tested the instrument. Free to make the most of the minute, I hoped I might be delayed. "I'm leaving tomorrow morning. Write a letter to me and give it to me before eight o'clock tonight." I presented her with the package, and some tea and sugar. I understood her hatred; I saw failure ahead. But the partial concession succeeded. She puzzled over my speech. With arrogance, soundlessly, her eyes rested; the gloom, the light, close to my hand. She pulled my coat, her breath dry, rapid. "You often said you would leave. I accept it. I want you to stay. I cannot force you."

With pellets of light thudding overhead, she held a needle; we were huddled in a shelter – wet planks, rope, the copper light beat high above, which the eyes, the smoke, the wind, glimpsed above – we ducked for shelter. "You'll be glad to get home." I steered her away from the track with my hand; it was impossible. "You tell me how much – what power the state has." "I wouldn't know." "Have you thought about it?" "It's different now. Of course I'm against war, genuine war." Smoke flew past with a white hand, distinguishing marks – white numbers painted large. Empty huts; long hills shone with oil. Her glance went to the town with its menacing platforms, barracks, roofs, furnaces. I planned that she should. Without a smile, she shifted her position, leant towards the curved and slatted sun, completed her turn back to the walls of red stone, the sun now behind low cloud, through smoke, lines of streets, lines of trees, a spire hidden by smoke. I was home. My luggage would be taken down by car, unless I neglected altogether… "I can collect the stuff tomorrow." Her hand clutched. The smell of oil and smoke. A woman walked along the gutter, her grey face bleeding from scratches. A statue; her silence blocked the exit; there was no room. Flags, letters; I hoped to be home – the sky filled with familiar buildings; this visit would be made. There were two trains leaving at about the same time. I made sure that the luggage was sent on the first – it would be well looked after. Of course this visit had to be made. I had two hours, and during the whole of that time it would be necessary for me to shave and dress. My luggage contained my notes. When I unpacked, these were not to be found – they had been mislaid en route.

# Chapter 14

S HE LIVED CLOSE BY. A green-painted lamp with
rust on it, a dozen narrow steps, zinc handrails either
side, a table, steaming food, a dark place, bright metal
and white plates, the staircase leading away. I turned my
back. "Eat in this place?" I said loudly, stopped suddenly, interrupted. "It is, is it? Terrible?" Then her terror
disappeared; she behaved as though she were welcoming
me home – she referred to the food: "When did you last
eat?" "I haven't eaten. I'm not hungry." To save trouble,
she said, I should take my meals in the restaurant, set
out on a cloth. I guessed why. I nodded towards the
stairway. "Is there anyone here tonight?" "The person
who has been sharing the room left yesterday." It would
be possible for me to have my old room back, but I must
understand why, and on what conditions. I said I had
hoped to return home with her, after what I had seen.
"It's late in the month," she sniffed. "One returning
after so long should expect this particular difficulty.
Everybody comes, and stays for days – a whole week
at a time; you should see the crowds we have in this
house." I picked up my possessions and began to climb
the stairs. "You can have half, then." "A man doesn't
come back for half."

The door was open; light filtered through dirty windows. The room was adequate. Fireplace, table facing
windows, against the wall by the door a side table
with necessities on it. Four chairs. Beyond the small

table, a cupboard in which, among rubbish stuffed away, were two painted jugs, a cup decorated with the figure of Frederick the Great, a plate with a ship painted on it, a note found in a drawer, a bundle of papers written in order to be left behind. I examined the windows of the room, the lamp on which green letters were painted, attachments decorated with imitation leaves.

Staring idiotically at the closed door, I listened to two conversations continuing simultaneously. A man saying: "Not like you. The injustices, the iniquities of the system." Her soft reply: "I'm not saying which one I would choose." She sounded frightened; the door crashed open; her face showed in the doorway; she lost her balance; her shoulder fall was broken by the room, her face on the floor, flushed to the forehead. Light, bright light – yellow in the dark-looking burdened home. I followed, rested my knee on the curved window seat; ugly foundations of the old house – a tombstone from the old building. "We should celebrate my return." "Tell me, what do you think of yourself?" My reputation for being uncommunicative about either my movements or my amusements would not let me reply. Illuminated by the moon, she smiled. I held a fold of her skirt. "Leave me alone." I held a fold of sacking, looked down at the face of a child, ghastly with life, strong, violent. Betrayed, I sharply instructed her; she became frozen; I lost patience, I became an actor; she quiet, simple, cruel – an unhappy child shaped by the shape of a fall. "You killed." She went for my cheeks with her nails; I tried to grab her – she got to the window, tried to leap out. "Murderer!" I dragged her back, put my hand over her mouth. I turned off the light.

Next morning she had a scab on her wrist – she stared in surprise; she was sick. The house was bright with daylight. She was unable to move – she said her back was broken – she lay with wide face asleep, without a word. I understood what had happened.

After three days I called the state doctor. He came gorgeously in gold buttons. He was worse than a priest. He wrapped her in sheets – sheets soaked in icy water. He made her stand; he ordered pills and massage. She wanted me to nurse her. She was choking to the point of suffocation. The heart was bad. She feared the knife. I rushed out of the room, listened through the half-open door. It was too late. He wrapped a blanket round the child to save its life. I banged the door shut. I remained by the side of the bed, watching the terror. The operation would help. She nodded. An envelope on the table under the lamp told me that she had received that morning... there was no time for discussion. He decided to inject. The reaction was terrific. The body sprang up in a violent fit, bleeding from the nose. The condition improved. It was intensely interesting to watch the case. The child must be removed or the mother would die. I knew of no suitable place. The arrangements were inadequate. The doctor ordered it to be removed. In the morning it had gone. I dared not tell her; I decided to wait. The body was taken and buried. I nearly fell. It must be buried. It was impossible; it was forbidden by law. The body must be burnt. I asked what would be the price for a first-class funeral and grave. Times were hard – there had been a rise in the price of coffins. Ten thousand would cover everything – flowers would be extra. I arranged to have the body burnt – it was against the law to embalm or otherwise preserve the body. The certificate was signed; the cause of death was the heart. The sum paid in advance would have saved its life. I visited it; I had reasons. The night was dark with rain; my foot against the soft earth; I fell. Neither wanted to tell her. She knew. She had been sitting up in bed; she thought she was dead, and said she had died – looked straight and knew. She wanted to write a letter to her father accusing herself; I told her such a letter might make her father crazy. The next morning she was carried down and taken home. She presented the nurse with two big trunks full of clothes, and a hat. I persuaded her to keep the hat. I spent an hour on my knees in the room, on the floor in a spare room – I can still see the carpet. I told her I was all right. I wanted sleep. My brain dropped. I was asleep. The bell rang. I heard her voice. She was standing on the table in her short white skirt and embroidered bolero, painting her eyes and her mouth. She asked me how much money there was in my wallet – she needed some of the cash at once as she had come to the end of her savings. I told her the wallet was empty, but I offered to loan her some money if she wished, and gave her my personal cheque. She borrowed from me several times, and I was told she borrowed from others. She developed a mania for economy, forbade the lighting of fires, and at each purchase of food she complained bitterly. I entrusted her with the dispatch of my reports, but rather than spend money on telegrams she sent them by ordinary post, though she knew that the messages were for immediate publication. I was accustomed to cigars of the highest quality, but she bought the cheapest and wrapped them in silver paper. I threw them onto the fire.

She had been years in the grave. I remembered her long curls, but now they were faded. She could not live again. But she found friends. Two middle-aged ladies began to take an interest in her. They took her out for walks with them. It became an unnatural thing. She fell in love with them. Then she sent them flowers, and they were returned burnt, and, with them, her note torn in pieces. With her memories of the dead she caused bitter suffering; she had no friends; in the night she cried terribly. She offended many people. She told them too plainly what she saw.

Only her father continued to welcome her. He gave her a job to do. Her duty was to read him the papers. She concentrated on the press reports of crime and scandal — these were the matters, rather than the famine which had set in, which interested him. He demanded her constant presence throughout the day, and refused to allow her time to prepare my meals. She grew tired of the work, and became devoted to little dogs and to plants. She brought home an object found in the street — a puppy sewn up in the skin of an animal. When he met her carrying two plants she had bought in the town, her father startled her by calling out: "Two lovers in her arms!" Their arguments grew, and they turned to me for an opinion, which I declined to give.

I climbed the hill towards the bridge, aware of the threats which shadowed my life. She refused to join me. I ate solitary, extravagantly, pouring on my plate the remains of her food — three large spoonsful. I stopped at two o'clock, torn between knowledge. My work to do. Her desire to sleep. I left the decision to her. "Do as you please. If you go out, do not come back a minute later than half-past two." "I shan't go far. I'll take a walk to the bridge."

The bridge had a hut by the entrance. The wooden-sided structure was divided into three – one part waited with benches, the other shivered and muttered – the other was interesting, with coloured bottles. I took the key from a hook near the door. One corner of the hut fulfilled many purposes. Its outer part, where the wall projected, served as a store for board and pegs. Coal was stored there. Beneath the windows, a carpenter's bench. I touched the teeth of the saw, the cutting edge of a chisel. Her father had spent hundreds of hours working in wood and the lighter forms of iron. I pressed my face against the chisel. She looked away. "Enjoying yourself?" The voice came from her lean face. "Haven't you had enough?" I ignored this attempt at humour. Her trembling increased. Her face shook. She said she had been on her way to see me, but had decided to keep away. "You said you wouldn't mind." "I never said that." "What have you been doing?" I asked her, for something to say. "Nothing much." With her head level with the second window, frightened of losing her balance, she started to look over her shoulder. She tried to stop in the right position, began to walk towards the mechanism; she tried to run but was unable to. "Funny way of running." "I suppose it is." "Are you coming?" I knew the signs. "Will you come for an hour?" "Longer than that."

I went down the hill, unsmiling. I could see the bridge; I gazed down at the sides of the deep water; I had seen the road beyond – the new road did not go forwards. Higher on this side of the bridge, level with the tank from which water was piped to the town, the road approached from the far side; the wide road, its animal feet moving, pulling, it died away in the reeds along the banks.

I waited for her. She appeared from the bridge. We went through the old pantomime – I behaving as though my purpose was to caress, her insistence that more was needed – until despite denials and protests, she found the hidden gifts. We decided to return. She accepted the invitation, said that the evenings were usually empty, and that evening she had wanted me to come. We agreed on a meeting place: at the foot of the slope as we came off the bridge. "Will we need to repair the house?" "See for yourself when you get into the place," she said serenely. I knew that, to begin with, new timber was needed. As the subject was of interest, before continuing to speak to her about it, I demanded an account of where she had been and whom she had seen. I could hear my voice thundering. My attitude terrified her. "I have been preparing for that question from the first. You know the story, the pattern, my family." She began to turn the handle of the mechanism. She went back towards the bridge, pulling me with her, climbing the hill until we were high above and then down till we were exactly level with the door of her house. The road ended; we had gone through a narrow tunnel, and so into the yard. We walked up a path, and here was a waterway – the river grew wider. Reaching ground level after slithering down a grassy slope, she turned back to look at the chimney on the roof of her house. Guided by an unknown law, she defined her need and the way of satisfying it. In a recess about a yard deep, on the left side, up three stone steps, was the doorway to her house. Opposite was another door. Inside, a flight of wooden steps led down to the stone floor – a small compartment shuttered on two sides, one shutter facing the bank, another being used for ashes. "You're lucky," I said. "Our levels are now equal," she began. Her speech became less precise every minute she remained inside the house. It was hot. "I cannot stay long. I have jobs to do. I wanted to go across the road for a chat. She was wiping her hands on her dress. "I've finished." She went; I was by myself. I wondered whether or not I should have spoken in confidence. I didn't know. Indecisive, I stared up at the lines which crossed to connect the two buildings. The cellar had been long unused. It was not likely that she would come back.

# Chapter 15

I PASSED OVER THE PLANK spanning the brook – a tributary of the river – skirted the swampy ground, climbed down to avoid a gang of boys playing a dangerous game, a suicidal game. I climbed over a gate. Rows of gardens, rows of houses faced the lane. I knocked on the lowest door. Her father. Strong, bare arms. He was not pleased. He saw me. He looked at me and thought nothing.

"Her things are stored in her room." He sent me into her room. I found the things there. As I collected her clothes, he followed me about the room. He wandered into a long discourse which I had some difficulty in following. "You work – perhaps I too will work. I'm not unhappy. Soon we will all think of nothing; there will be a new world. She had a mother – she tried to talk. She said: don't judge, don't experience, don't try to get away, only doctors know the causes of diseases. Now this girl, she's a child, don't deny it, like it. I don't think there will be a war, but it may all end." He looked suddenly old. "We did not know how to live. We fought – we had to fight; it was simple – that was all there was. That's not true – appearances lie; it was for nothing – our revolution was one of the most insignificant; we used big words. My useful time was when I lived with my wife; we had a small flat, ordinary chairs, played hide-and-seek with work – there was dust over everything soon enough. Her eyes were always tired; she knew what she was. I heard it said – 'your wife seems tired' – and my reply, 'not really'. Her womb twisted over, choked by work. She used to listen to the wireless. I was too busy; she was old and leading an empty life; she never had the windows open – she begged me not to open them. No basin, no proper clothes; she was lying on the bed covered by a coat. She was in pain, she needed medicine, she couldn't eat. I was very, very tired. We could not afford a doctor. When the ulcers burst, I was bathing the baby. In those days I could do a lot; now I haven't the patience – I am unable to move or think. We never went out. She had kidney trouble. Two children died. Three children – two died. And the girl, you know, has been operated on." "I didn't know." "My wife would have looked after you. She had to do all the lifting – she had to shovel, carry coke; those were the hardest days. I blame myself. Because of my work, nights and days of fighting and planning, she had to lift things. She injured her spine – it gave her pains in her shoulders; she should have stayed in bed, but she would not do so. She felt acute pain, but her horror of hospitals was stronger than the pain. There was no remedy, only stupidity and ignorance. I am damp and old. There was no one to lead them – no one who would die. My son fought and was killed. I saw him fall. All he could do was die. In those few hours, I hope he was suitably drugged – probably not. Now there is nothing. No one stays alive; he has died – his house is in ruins because of the chains on his legs. He was made to run over loose flints during great heat, allowed to fetch water but forbidden to drink it. He was isolated – the windows of his hut were nailed up and painted over. He was made to lie inside on his plank bed all day and all night, except for one hour when he was

taken out for their pleasure. It was not possible for him
to keep his own cup and plate. There were no bedclothes
on his bed. There was no gas stove or oven, no meat safe.
His room had bare boards, little warmth; the bed was
badly broken, very damp and cold. The floor was earth;
the plaster had fallen from the walls; vermin nested there.
The opening to the air was on one side only – so narrow
that ventilation was impossible. In front of the opening,
sewage stood, and a pit over which the air that entered
the room had to pass. The liquid which drained from the
pit seeped through the earth and lay in pools by the walls
of the room. The surface of the water was polluted, the
ground saturated with the foul liquid which darkened the
walls and ran beneath the floor, soaking the boards. There
was no stove, no decent cupboards; a kettle with a broken
spout; two bowls with holes stopped up with rags. The
floor was bare stone. The mattress was broken. The room
had no furniture besides the bed. The room was empty.
No gas stove or oven. We had two lead spoons – fingers
were used for eating; no basins – we could not drink tea.
Inside the air was bad, and he became unconscious. He
was strapped down to a block, his head muffled in blankets. He was given twenty-five lashes with a whip which
had been left soaking in water for the purpose since the
preceding day. They took it in turns to beat him. He was
hung up on a post with his hands tied behind his back so
that with his toes he could just touch the ground. He was
sent to a dark cell and given fifty lashes; he was forced to
run with his barrow full of stones. He was not allowed to
move. He was told he could not be free for twenty years.
You will never come out. Coloured stripes were sewn on
his clothes for shame – red bands perpendicular on the

back, yellow stripes with red circles, red bands crossed, red bands with yellow circles, red bands with blue circles, blue bands, perpendicular yellow stripes striped on his back. They got tired of tormenting him. He was made to work in a water-filled ditch – forced with blows beneath the surface. When he crawled out he was forced back – forced to crawl on his knees; made to stand while others ate; given twenty strokes of the lash – a tapering thong of cowhide. He was strapped to a trestle. He seized a hammer and tried to brain himself, but was stopped. He tried to hang himself, but they saw it and he was saved. He sharpened a piece of tin and opened the arteries in both arms. A load of stones was tipped over him."

I walked back towards the house. I paused to lean over the wall where the camp had been. Building was in progress. I continued to the bridge, where, on turning, I saw her, far away, approaching. Fifty yards farther on, we met. "I saw your father this morning." "I know. He told me you would go there. He's hardly a father. A friend. But a friend for years." Slow speaking, slow thinking. "I wish he could have more fresh air. He works long hours; he needs more air than his long days permit." "He's by himself at home, like you." "The same. Yet he's a man – a man whom a woman could desire for a husband."

We went home to the cutting of wood, the laying and lighting of the fire, smoke from the fire, amused manoeuvrings, her pulse beating in her neck, though she was conscious only that the hours were wasted.

# Note on the Text

The text in the present volume is based on the first edition of *Europe after the Rain*, published by John Calder (Publishers) Ltd in 1965. The spelling and punctuation in the text have been anglicized, standardized, modernized and made consistent throughout.

The unusual paragraphing in the text – speakers following one another in the same paragraph – has been replicated from the first edition in order to follow the author's wishes as closely as possible, preserving the aleatoric device and his professed wish to "cock a snook at the body of traditional literature".

# CALDER PUBLICATIONS
## EDGY TITLES FROM A LEGENDARY LIST

*Heliogabalus,*
*or The Anarchist Crowned*
Antonin Artaud

*Babel*
Alan Burns

*Buster*
Alan Burns

*Celebrations*
Alan Burns

*Dreamerika!*
Alan Burns

*Europe after the Rain*
Alan Burns

*Changing Track*
Michel Butor

*Moderato Cantabile*
Marguerite Duras

*The Garden Square*
Marguerite Duras

*Selected Poems*
Paul Éluard

*The Blind Owl
and Other Stories*
Sadeq Hedayat

*The Bérenger Plays*
Eugène Ionesco

*Six Plays*
Luigi Pirandello

*Eclipse:
Concrete Poems*
Alan Riddell

*A Regicide*
Alain Robbe-Grillet

*In the Labyrinth*
Alain Robbe-Grillet

*Jealousy*
Alain Robbe-Grillet

*The Erasers*
Alain Robbe-Grillet

*The Voyeur*
Alain Robbe-Grillet

*Locus Solus*
Raymond Roussel

*Impressions of Africa*
Raymond Roussel

*Tropisms*
Nathalie Sarraute

*Politics and Literature*
Jean-Paul Sartre

*The Wall*
Jean-Paul Sartre

*The Flanders Road*
Claude Simon

*Cain's Book*
Alexander Trocchi

*The Holy Man*
*and Other Stories*
Alexander Trocchi

*Young Adam*
Alexander Trocchi

*Seven Dada Manifestos*
*and Lampisteries*
Tristan Tzara